"Gwen, are you all right?" Dean asked.

Gwen looked up at him with tear-filled eyes, and his stomach tightened at how often he'd been the cause of her tears in the past. She had once said she would never forgive him, and he believed her.

He wished he could let her know how he regretted that, but now was not the time to tell her.

She nodded. "When I smelled that gasoline, I was so scared. Then I thought I was the only one who'd survived the wreck."

Dean smiled. "But you called 911 anyway. That was quick thinking."

Her cheeks flushed, and a smile pulled at her lips. "I'm just glad that your cell phone fell out of your pocket."

Their stilted conversation reminded him of how different things were now between the two of them compared to what they'd been years ago. How he wished he could go back and tell that young police officer to do things differently, but he couldn't.

"Gwen, I—" he began, then stopped as someone approached them.

What was done, was done, and the past couldn't be changed.

But the present could.

Sandra Robbins is an award-winning, multipublished author of Christian fiction who lives with her husband in Tennessee. Without the support of her wonderful husband, four children and five grandchildren, it would be impossible for her to write. It is her prayer that God will use her words to plant seeds of hope in the lives of her readers so they may come to know the peace she draws from her life.

Books by Sandra Robbins

Love Inspired Suspense

Smoky Mountain Secrets

In a Killer's Sights

Bounty Hunters

Fugitive Trackdown
Fugitive at Large
Yuletide Fugitive Threat

The Cold Case Files

Dangerous Waters
Yuletide Jeopardy
Trail of Secrets

Visit the Author Profile page at Harlequin.com.

IN A KILLER'S SIGHTS

SANDRA ROBBINS

HARLEQUIN® LOVE INSPIRED® SUSPENSE

Recycling programs
for this product may
not exist in your area.

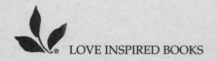

LOVE INSPIRED BOOKS

ISBN-13: 978-0-373-44754-1

In a Killer's Sights

Copyright © 2016 by Sandra Robbins

Come now, and let us reason together, saith the Lord: though your sins be as scarlet, they shall be as white as snow; though they be red like crimson, they shall be as wool.
–*Isaiah* 1:18

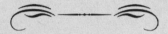

Dedicated to Kylie, who gave me the idea for
setting a story on a dude ranch in the Smoky Mountains

ONE

Gwen Anderson planted her feet in a wide stance and stared down into the crystal clear waters of the Great Smoky Mountains stream twenty feet below. Late afternoon sunlight filtered through the fall foliage, casting shadows across the water. Her position provided the perfect photo op for her research. In a few months, she would begin producing a documentary about the most visited national park in the country for WNT, a New York–based television network.

Her camera hung on a strap around her neck, and she raised it to her eyes. A strand of hair slipped out of her metal hair clip and wedged itself in front of the viewfinder. With a sigh, she adjusted the clip and tugged on it to make sure it was anchored in place. Then she raised the camera and peered through it, scanning the terrain below in an effort to get the best shot.

As she inched closer to the edge, she stepped on a loose rock she hadn't seen in the moss, and her foot slipped. With a scraping sound, the rock tumbled downward. She cringed at the sound of it knocking against the limestone face and releasing a small avalanche of other stones. For a moment she teetered on the edge of the cliff, thinking she might very well follow them, but then she steadied herself.

The thud of stones striking the ground reached her ears, but it was another sound that made her breath hitch in her throat. A surprised cry rang out from below. The thought that a hiker or camper had been on the riverbank and was injured by one of the falling rocks set her heart to pounding. Dreading what she'd see, Gwen stepped carefully to the brink and stared down.

Her eyes widened in shock at the sight below. A man dressed in camouflage, with a body draped over his shoulder, stood at the edge of the water and stared up at her. Although the black ski mask he wore covered his face, his eyes glared at her through the slits of his disguise.

Neither of them moved for a few seconds as they gazed at each other. Then, with a shove, he dumped the body into the rushing water. Gwen watched in horror as it bobbed a few times before the current carried it away downstream.

Instinct kicked in, and she raised the camera and snapped a picture, just as the man lifted his arm—with a gun in his hand. A moment later, the sound of a gunshot echoed in the valley. Pieces of shattered rock exploded around her as the bullet struck inches from where she stood, making her flinch back automatically and squeeze her eyes shut. She took a deep breath and peered through the viewfinder once more, but the man was no longer there.

Panic welled up in her. It was time to get to safety. Her car sat at the trailhead parking lot a mile away, and she needed to head there now. Careful not to slip on the mossy rocks, Gwen scrambled toward the trail as fast as she could. Once there she took off running, but she could hear the sound of someone sprinting behind her.

Knowing her life depended on it, she pushed her body to move faster, to outrun the killer, who sounded as if he was gaining on her with every step. The deserted trail stretched ahead, and she groaned, unsure she could make it all the way to the parking lot before she collapsed—or got caught by her pursuer.

What should she do? Continue on, or take her chances in the forest on either side of the path? Of the two, the forest seemed the better choice. Although the vegetation would slow her progress some, she might be able to find a hiding place in the dense woods. Before she could decide, another gunshot sounded, and bark on a tree to the right of the trail exploded in small fragments.

Her nostrils flared in fear as she realized he'd gained even more ground and it would be only a matter of time before he caught up to her. Already she was weakening, and her chest was heaving as she gasped for air. The better choice was to take her chances off the trail. Veering right, she plunged into the thick forest and wove among the tree trunks.

The heavy footsteps slowed a bit, but didn't stop.

Now they were crashing over the fallen limbs and leaves that littered the ground. And worst of all, he was still right behind her.

There had to be somewhere she could hide. But where? The trees in this part of the forest were too small to conceal a figure behind them, and she wasn't close enough to the hillside to find a cave. Just when she was about to give up hope, she spotted a large rotting tree off to her left, a big hollow in its trunk. She didn't know if she could fit into it or not, but needed to try. Her pursuer would catch up to her any minute.

With a burst of speed, Gwen raced to the tree. Her research had told her that black bears in the Smokies liked to hibernate in hollowed-out trees, and if this was a bear's den, she hoped no one was home today. Swallowing the bile that poured into her mouth, she dropped down on her hands and knees and scurried into the gaping hole.

She wiggled in and pressed her body against the back side of the trunk. With any luck the man from the stream wouldn't see her. The sound of approaching footsteps crashing through the forest caused her to stiffen and hold her breath. He came closer and then ran on by without stopping.

She waited a few minutes, catching her breath, before she crawled out and looked around. He was nowhere in sight, and she couldn't hear him running. Taking a deep gulp of air, she turned and ran.

What felt like endless moments later, she was back on the trail and racing toward the parking lot. If she could just get to her car, she could get away. Then she'd go to the sheriff's department and take her camera. She wasn't sure if the picture of a man's face hidden by a ski mask would be helpful or not, but there might be another way to identify him. And a way to find out who his victim was.

When the parking lot came into sight, she breathed a sigh of relief and urged her tired body to jog the last few feet to where her car was parked. She was almost there when she heard a shout behind her.

"Stop! Or I'll shoot!"

Gwen glanced over her shoulder, and her legs almost collapsed at what she saw. The man, still wearing the ski mask, ran from the woods, his gun aimed at her. Her car sat no more than twenty feet away. He was at least twice that distance. Should she stop or try for the vehicle?

Before she even knew what she had decided, she willed her legs into a new burst of speed and barreled toward her car. A shot rang out and struck beside her foot on the paved parking lot. She gasped, but didn't stop.

She was almost to the car when another shot rang out and bounced off the fender. The sound of the ricochet sent terror flowing through her, and she stumbled. Her arms flailed the air as she fell forward, landing facedown on the asphalt. The strap holding her camera around her neck broke, and the device skidded across the parking lot, out of reach.

Gwen scrambled to get up, but by then the killer stood a few feet away with the weapon pointed at her. His eyes blazed with anger through the slits of the mask, and his chilling laugh sent shivers up her spine. Without taking the gun off her, he slowly reached down and picked up her camera.

"Well, well," he snarled. "Thought you could get away from me? It looks like today's not your day."

Gwen pushed herself into a sitting position and scooted backward until she felt the door of her car behind her. "Please," she begged. "I don't know who you are, and I won't say anything. Just please don't hurt me."

He chuckled again and shook his head. "You should have thought of that before you became so nosy."

She raised her hands in front of her as if they could shield her from a bullet. "There's no need to do this."

"Sorry," he said and raised the gun.

Gwen closed her eyes to say a quick prayer for those she loved and would leave behind, but snapped them open again at the sound of a voice shouting from nearby. "What's going on here?"

Her assailant whirled and stared at the road to the parking lot. Gwen's heart slammed against her chest as she spied horses with riders in single file—a trail ride. The leader spurred his mount forward, and she cringed against the car, waiting to see what would happen next.

The man in the mask appeared to waver, uncertain. He retreated a step, pointed the gun at the rider and then back at her. He gave a strangled cry and then fired. Gwen sat there, stunned, as she felt something wet trickle down her face. Puzzled, she reached up, touched the side of her head and felt blood. With a groan, she toppled forward. The rough pavement scraped her cheek, and she heard the hoofbeats of a horse speeding past. Then darkness settled over her, and she slipped into unconsciousness.

Dean Harwell hadn't counted on stumbling on a crime in progress when he'd led his dude-ranch guests on their first trail ride in the Smokies. But despite his surprise, he didn't hesitate to act.

Years of service as a police officer served him well as he spurred his horse toward the gunman in an effort to save the woman's life. His heart dropped to the pit of his stomach when the man aimed and fired at her. Out of the corner of his eye Dean saw her slump facedown on the pavement before the man turned and ran into the woods.

His foreman, Emmett Truitt, rode up beside him. "Did we just witness a murder, Dean?"

"Looks like it," he replied. "The shooter's gone into the forest. I can't risk injury to my horse by taking him in there. Call 911 for the woman, and I'll go after him."

He dismounted, threw the reins to Emmett and plunged into the forest after the fleeing gunman. After about a half mile he stopped and listened. No sounds came from around him. Even the birds had chosen to go quiet. He hadn't caught sight of the man even once since following him into the woods, and he couldn't hear anyone running.

It was time to admit he'd lost the trail. With a sigh, Dean turned around and retraced his steps to the parking lot. When he got there, emergency vehicles, their lights flashing, were scattered across the parking lot.

An ambulance with its back door open appeared to be ready to transport the victim. Sheriff Ben Whitman, Dean's friend since they'd met in middle school years ago, stood beside his police car talking to one of his deputies.

Even from this distance it was easy to see Ben's Cherokee heritage in his high cheekbones, coarse black hair and reddish skin tone. They'd played football together, double-dated and shared confidences since they were kids. But it was what Ben had done for him in the past five years that meant the most. He had been Dean's sponsor when he'd entered an alcohol rehabilitation program, and Ben was the main reason he'd been successful in overcoming his addiction.

When Ben spotted Dean, he hurried over. "Did you see where he went?"

Dean shook his head. "He disappeared as soon as he left the parking lot. He must know these woods well to get away so quickly." He glanced at the gurney where the woman lay, with EMT Joe Collins and another man in scrubs bent over her, administering aid.

Only her feet were visible. It was impossible to tell how badly she might be hurt. "Is she dead?"

"No," Ben said. "She's unconscious, though. The paramedics are about ready to transport her."

Dean craned his neck to get a better look at the woman, but still couldn't see her face. "How badly is she hurt?" he asked.

Ben tugged at the brim of his hat to straighten it. "Not nearly as bad as we thought at first. Emmett and your guests said they saw a man with a gun aimed right at her head when he fired. The only thing that saved her life was a big metal hair clip she had on. The bullet apparently struck it and bounced off. Grazed her head when it ricocheted and the wound bled quite a bit, but she's going to be fine."

"I guess God was watching out for her today," Dean said. "When I rode up and saw the guy about to shoot her, I thought it was a robbery gone bad. Was it?"

"That was my first thought, but I won't know until I can talk with her. The impact of the bullet knocked her out, and she hasn't regained consciousness yet."

"Have you ever seen her around before?"

Ben shook his head. "Probably a tourist. She's in a rental car. We found a wallet in her jeans pocket and her driver's license is from New York. I'm guessing she may have encountered her attacker on the trail or in the parking lot and was trying to get away from him when you arrived."

Dean nodded. "That makes sense. Maybe she just happened to be in the wrong place at the wrong time."

"That's what I'm thinking," Ben said before he stared off into the woods. "I'm going to call in some guys to help us search this area on the chance that we might find something that points to our shooter. Want to come along?"

Dean nodded again. "I'll be glad to. I'll take my guests to the ranch and come on back."

"Good. There's not a guide around that knows

these mountains like you do," his friend stated. "I sure am glad you came back home to live. Now, if you'd give up that dude ranch and come work for me, I'd be perfectly happy."

Dean frowned at that. "My days of being a police officer are over. I loved it until I…" He paused and stared down at the wedding ring he'd never been able to take off. "Well, you know some of what happened. It ruined my life for a time."

"But you overcame everything."

Dean sighed and raked his hand through his hair. "Not everything, buddy. There are some people I never will get the chance to make it up to. People who I've had to learn to live without. One especially."

Ben clamped his hand on Dean's shoulder. "You know I've always been glad to listen to you about what happened, but I know there's a lot you've never told me. When you're ready, I'm willing to hear."

Dean smiled briefly. "Thanks. I'll remember that." Then he took a deep breath. "Now I'd better get these guests home so I can come help you with the search."

"See you later," Ben said before he turned and walked to his cruiser.

Dean started to head to where Emmett stood, but noticed the EMTs were about to load the woman in the ambulance and detoured to check on her. He walked over and stopped behind Joe. "How's she doing?" he asked.

The paramedic glanced over his shoulder and smiled. "Still passed out, but she's going to be fine. If that bullet had been a half inch to the left of that hair clip, we'd be taking her body to the county coroner's office instead of the hospital."

"That's what Ben said. And he said she's from New York."

Joe nodded. "Yeah. She's a long way from home. I wonder what she's doing in the Smokies all alone."

Dean frowned. "Maybe she isn't alone. Did Ben find anything that would tell where she's staying while she's here? Maybe a key card from a hotel or a receipt from a cabin rental company?"

"Not that I know of."

Dean glanced to the far side of the parking lot. Emmett and two of his employees seemed to have everything under control with the horses and guests, but it would be dinnertime soon. They needed to get back to the ranch for the cookout that was planned for the evening. "Well, I'd better get these folks back to my ranch, and you need to get her to the hospital. I hope everything turns out well for her." He stepped around Joe and was about to leave when he glanced down and saw the woman's face for the first time.

His eyes opened wide, and a strangled cry came from his throat as a shock like an electrical current raced through his body. His legs wobbled, and he staggered and would have fallen if Joe hadn't grabbed his arm and steadied him.

"Dean! Are you okay?"

He could hear Joe's voice, but couldn't respond. The words Dean tried to say got tangled in his throat, and a strange gurgling emerged. He stared down at the woman, his heart pounding as if he'd just run a marathon.

No! It can't be.

Joe clasped his arm more tightly and shook him. "Dean! Dean! I asked if you're all right."

He bent over and propped his hands on his knees, gulping great breaths of air in an effort to calm his racing pulse. "No, I'm not," he rasped.

With a strangled cry, he dropped to his knees and touched the bandage that covered the wound on her head. Just a few inches and she'd be dead. And he'd run right past her when he'd rushed into the woods. Why hadn't he stopped to see if she needed help?

She looked so pale. Blood matted her blond hair, which he gently smoothed back from her eyes. "Gwen," he crooned. "Can you hear me? It's Dean."

Her left hand rested on the sheet that covered her body. He grasped it and rubbed his thumb down her ring finger. He could still feel the indentation at the base where she'd once worn a ring, but it wasn't there now.

Ben must have seen his reaction, because he dropped down beside him. "Dean, do you know this woman?"

Guilt and sorrow welled up and flooded his soul like a tidal wave. Dean closed his eyes for a moment and took a deep breath. "Ben, it's Gwen. It's my wife."

TWO

Ben gasped and a shocked look covered his face. "I saw on her driver's license that her name was Gwen Anderson, but I didn't think about this being your ex-wife. You know I was in the army when the two of you married, and I never met her. In fact, I don't think you ever showed me a picture of her." He stared at Gwen for a moment and exhaled. "So she took back her maiden name?"

Dean swallowed and squeezed her hand tighter. "Yeah. I guess she didn't want anything to remind her of me."

Ben dropped his palm on Dean's shoulder. "Man, I know this is a shock, but don't let it throw you too badly."

Before he could answer, Joe interrupted. "We need to get her to the hospital so the doctor can check her over."

Dean didn't want to let go of Gwen's hand. It had been so long since he'd touched her, and once she regained consciousness, she wouldn't allow him that privilege. But she needed to get to the hospital. With a sigh, he released it and backed away from the gurney so the EMTs could get her inside.

"Okay, but I'm going in the ambulance with her."

Joe glanced at the other paramedic, who shrugged in agreement. "Okay," Joe said, "but move out of the way and let us get her loaded. Then you can climb in with her."

Ben patted Dean on the back. "I need to check on the search my deputies are doing, but I'll see you at the hospital later."

He nodded and then motioned to Emmett, who hurried across the lot, a perplexed expression on his face. "You look like you've seen a ghost, boss. Is something wrong?"

Dean bit down on his lip and debated how much he should reveal to his foreman. After a moment he sighed. "Yeah." He hitched in a breath. "I know the woman who was hurt, and I'm going to the hospital with her. Will you take my horse back to the ranch? I'll call you when I'm ready to come home, so somebody can come get me."

Emmett glanced toward the gurney, then back to Dean. "Okay. Anything else?"

"I won't be there for the guest cookout tonight, so you'll need to help my grandfather with it. Is that a problem for you?"

"No problem. We can handle it. But how long do you think you'll be?"

Dean had no idea. He might not be at the hospital long. It all depended on what Gwen had to say when she regained consciousness, whenever that might be. "I'm not sure. I'll phone and let you know."

Before Emmett could say anything else, Joe's voice rang out from the rear of the ambulance. "Dean, if you're going with us, come on. We're ready to leave."

He nodded and climbed into the vehicle. The gurney took up more than half the space inside, and Dean squeezed in beside Gwen as Joe moved to close the ambulance door. When it was secured, he yelled to his partner, "We're ready to go back here. Are you sure you wouldn't rather I drive?"

"No, thanks. I've got this," the man called back.

Joe shrugged and tried to control the smile that pulled at his mouth. "Wilson is new, and he's not used to navigating these mountain roads yet, but he really wants to prove himself. Still, I'm a little concerned about him taking this one. You know how those steep curves can cause a driver to lose control, and there aren't any guardrails."

Dean nodded. "Yeah, I've heard some horror stories about this stretch. But if this guy is going to work around here, he'd better get used to it. No getting around the fact that we live in the mountains."

Joe chuckled. "You're right about that." He picked up the blood-pressure cuff, leaned in and wrapped it around Gwen's arm. When he'd finished the procedure, he nodded. "Looks good."

Then he scooted out of the way, leaving Dean access to Gwen again. He took her hand in one of his and stroked his thumb across her knuckles as his other hand brushed her hair back behind her ear. For a few seconds all he did was stare down at her, quenching the longing he'd had to see her again. She hadn't changed much in the past five years. Her hair wasn't as long as it used to be, but still felt as silky as when he'd first met her.

Pert was the word he and her friends had used to describe her back then. He wondered if she was still that sassy girl he'd loved or if the years had jaded her as they had him.

Eight years ago she'd been an assistant to the news staff at WLMT radio in Oxford, a town near Nashville. He'd been a police officer then. He remembered so well the night he first saw her. He'd been working on a case involving a serial killer who had chosen Gwen and her friend C.J. as his next victims. Dean had found her at the radio station locked in a closet waiting for the killer who'd left her there as he attempted to dispose of her friend. When he'd opened that door and seen how terrified she was, she had become more than a victim to him.

But it was her strength afterward, her determination not to let her horrible experience wear her down, that had won him over. Her vibrant spirit refused to be dimmed, and it had dazzled him. She had stolen his heart.

They'd been married six months later. And over the next two years, even though it was the last thing he ever would have wanted, he'd succeeded where the killer had failed and crushed some of her bright optimism.

Dean should have known better than to have subjected her to the problems in his life. As much as he'd loved her, he hadn't been able to keep the demons of his past from destroying the best thing that had ever happened to him. She'd tried to save their marriage, but at the time he couldn't meet her halfway. Now, for some reason, he'd been given the chance to see her again, and he didn't know if this was what he wanted or not.

Gwen stirred on the gurney, and Dean tightened his grip on her hand, silently willing her to wake up. The thought had no sooner entered his head than he questioned his decision to get in the ambulance. He had no idea if she would be happy to see him. Probably not. The day their divorce had been finalized, she'd told him in no uncertain terms that she didn't want to ever hear from him again. She'd said she was leaving Oxford and that he should never try to find her.

He'd agreed and for the past five years had kept his promise. Now she'd suddenly reappeared, in the last place he would have expected.

As the ambulance sped along the mountain road, he said a prayer of thanks that she'd come through her ordeal alive. Dean wanted to pray that she would be happy to see him when she woke up, but that probably wasn't going to happen.

Suddenly her eyes blinked open. "Wh-where am I?" she whispered.

Dean released her hand and scooted out of the way so Joe could lean over her.

"Miss Anderson," he said, "you're in an ambulance. We're on our way to the hospital. A doctor has been alerted and is waiting for us. Just relax, and we should be there in a few minutes."

She closed her eyes. "My head hurts," she murmured.

"I know. The doc will take care of that when we get to the hospital. Now just lie still."

She swallowed and looked up at him again. "Who are you?"

"My name's Joe. I'm one of the EMTs taking care of you."

Her eyes opened wide and she swallowed hard. Her body trembled as she tried to push herself up from the gurney. "Th-that man…"

Joe put his hands on her shoulders and eased her back down. "Don't think about that right now. The sheriff will want to talk to you later about what happened. For now, just relax and don't worry. You're safe."

She breathed a sigh of relief. "Thank you. You're very kind."

Joe glanced over his shoulder at Dean, who'd been holding his breath in suspense. "There's somebody here who wants to see you," the EMT said.

A frown pulled at her forehead. "Who?"

Joe moved out of the way, and Dean eased in next to the gurney. "It's me, Gwen."

For a moment she didn't move, and then a dazed look clouded her eyes. "No," she gasped. "This can't be real."

Dean smiled and covered her hand with his as he leaned closer. "Yes, it's real, Gwen. I'm here."

At his touch, her fingers stiffened. Then she pulled her hand free and turned her face away. "No, no, this can't be happening," she moaned.

She had to be dreaming. Dean had been out of her life for five years. How could he be staring down at her in the back of an ambulance? She closed her eyes in hopes of clearing his image from her mind and groaned again.

"Miss Anderson!" The EMT's voice penetrated the thick fog that seemed to be rolling into her brain, and she glanced up again. Dean no longer hovered over her. Now the young man who'd said his name was Joe was there. "Settle down, Miss Anderson. Don't get upset."

She tried to peer past him, to determine if she had really seen Dean's face or just imagined it, but Joe's body blocked her view. Her lips felt as if they were made of sandpaper when she licked them. "Dean?" Her voice wobbled as if she was begging the young man to assure her he was the only one with her.

Instead he smiled and nodded. "Yes, Dean's here. He says he's your husband. Is that right?"

"Ex-husband. Why is he here?"

Joe glanced over his shoulder and frowned. "I think you might need to answer that."

The paramedic stepped back from the gurney, and Gwen's stomach clenched when Dean maneuvered next to where she lay. "It's really you!" she said weakly. "I thought I was dreaming."

"No, you weren't dreaming."

He reached for her hand, but she pulled it away. The muscles in his throat constricted as he swallowed, his gaze raking her face.

He looked the same as he always had, yet different. Healthier. His face wasn't as bloated, nor was his complexion as red as the last time she'd seen him. His lips quirked up at the corners in a smile she remembered so well.

"I was leading a trail ride when I saw a man about to shoot you. Of course, I didn't know it was you at first. But he...but he—" Dean's voice cracked as if the words were lodged in his throat.

Her heart pricked at the way his eyes darkened. "I know. I remember him pointing the gun and firing. How could he have missed? He was so close to me."

"He didn't miss," Dean said. "There was a metal clip holding your hair back. The bullet hit it and bounced off. It saved your life."

She closed her eyes and shuddered. "I'm alive just because I put it in before I left the motel this morning?" She raised her hand and ran her fingers through her hair. When she didn't feel the clip, she frowned. "Where is it now?"

"The police took it for evidence." Dean leaned closer. "Had you ever seen this man before? Had he been following you, or did you just happen across him on the trail?"

She shook her head. "He was wearing a mask, so

I can't be sure, but I don't think I've ever laid eyes on him before I saw him dumping a body in the river. When he spotted me, he chased me back to the parking lot."

Dean's eyes grew wide with shock. "Dumping a body?"

"Yes. I took a picture of it, but then dropped my camera when I fell in the parking lot. Did the police find it?"

"No. It wasn't there."

She sighed. "That's too bad. I had a clear angle from where I was standing on the cliff above the stream."

Dean gasped. "Did this guy see you take the picture? Is that why he followed you?"

"Yes."

Dean raked his hand through his hair and gritted his teeth. "Gwen, you should have gotten out of there right away. You were married to a police officer long enough to know what happens when someone is witness to a crime."

She stared at him for a moment, the memory of how scared she'd been as she ran through the forest welling up in her mind. Her nostrils flared, and she tried again to push herself up from the gurney. "I think I learned a lot during that time," she spit out. "Maybe we should just say I was married to you *long enough*, and leave it at that."

Joe reached out and grasped Dean's shoulder. "Take it easy, man. She doesn't need to get upset."

Dean closed his eyes and took a deep breath. "I

wasn't criticizing you, Gwen. It scares me to think what almost happened to you. I'm sorry."

She blinked to keep tears from rolling down her cheeks and pressed her palm against her forehead. "I'm sorry, too, Dean. I shouldn't have reacted as I did."

Neither of them spoke for a moment, and then he sighed. "So, what are you doing in the Smokies?"

"I work for a television network in New York. We're going to do a documentary that features the Great Smoky Mountains National Park. I had hiked up to the stream to take some pictures for research."

He smiled. "New York, huh? You finally made the big time like you wanted."

"It's a good job," she said. "But what about you? I didn't think you'd ever come back to the Smokies."

He sighed and a sad smile curled his lips. "After the divorce, I decided I had to change something about my life. It was either get sober or die, and I chose to get sober. I turned my life over to God and got in a program for alcoholics. I haven't had a drink in four years."

Her mouth fell open in surprise. "That's wonderful, Dean! I'm so happy for you."

"I'm happy, too," he said. "I decided to come back where I grew up. My grandfather needed some help with his farm, and I found I missed the mountains. And it felt great to be sober. So I moved in with Granddad, and we decided to turn the farm into a dude ranch. It's doing very well."

She smiled. "It sounds like life has been good for you."

A sad expression darkened his eyes again. "My one regret was that you didn't know about it. But now you do."

"Now I do," she whispered.

Dean opened his mouth to speak, but before he could, a loud pop exploded outside the ambulance. The driver gave a startled cry as the vehicle swerved to the right, hit the loose gravel on the shoulder and veered back across the road.

"Wilson!" Joe yelled. "What's the matter?"

"I think we've been shot at!" he shouted, just as a second pop sounded.

Dean jumped to his feet and stared through the window that divided the back of the ambulance from the cab. "Are you hit?" he yelled.

"No, but I think a tire was. I'm losing control!"

The ambulance careened across the pavement, reached the other shoulder and plunged down the mountainside. Joe fell to the floor as compartments flew open and medical supplies tumbled out. Gwen screamed, and Dean grabbed her as she rolled from the gurney. They both dropped to the floor as the vehicle, picking up speed, bounced past trees and low-hanging limbs on its journey down the slope.

Gwen felt Dean's arms tighten around her as they crouched there, his body shielding hers. Then, without warning, the ambulance came to a jarring halt as it collided with something solid, most likely a tree or a rock.

The impact shook the vehicle with such force that she, Dean and Joe flew as if they'd been shot from a cannon into the walls and then back to the floor. She could hear the paramedic moaning near the panel at the front, but Dean lay next to her unmoving.

Frantic, she grabbed his shoulder and shook him. "Dean! Are you okay?" When he didn't answer, she shook him again. "Dean! Dean! Wake up."

A low moan came from Joe's direction. She tried to raise her head to see if he was conscious, but Dean's body blocked her view. "Joe! Are you okay?"

No answer. She tried calling out to the driver, too, but there was no response.

She pushed Dean's body off her and knelt next to him. A cell phone lay beside him, probably knocked from his pocket when he was thrown against the wall. She scooped it up and punched in the necessary numbers.

An operator answered right away. "This is 911. What is your emergency?"

"I need help!" Gwen screamed. "The ambulance that answered the call to White Oak Creek has crashed down the mountain. There are three others with me, but I'm the only one conscious right now."

"I have the ambulance on our GPS, and I've notified responders. They should be there soon. Who's there with you?"

"The driver. I think I heard that his name is Wilson? There's also an EMT named Joe, and Dean Harwell. Please tell the responders to hurry. I'm afraid the men are hurt badly."

"They're on the way. Stay on the line with me."

"I will, but please tell them…" The words froze in her throat at the smell that filled the ambulance. "Gasoline!" she screamed. "I smell gasoline."

"You need to get out of the ambulance now, ma'am." The woman's voice crackled over the cell phone.

"I can't leave them all here!" Gwen cried.

Before she could move, the back door of the vehicle opened. She recoiled at the sight of a man dressed in camouflage with a black ski mask over his face. He held a gun that he instantly aimed at her.

"Well, we meet again," he sneered, his words muffled by the mask.

"What do you want?" Gwen cried.

"What I *don't* want is for you to live to tell what you saw up on that mountain," he snarled.

Gwen held her hands in front of her and tried to scoot backward, but Joe's body blocked her. Beside her, Dean began to stir. "I don't know anything. I can't even see your face. Please put that gun down," she begged.

He laughed and took a step closer. "I can't take a chance. Sorry, lady." He slowly reached in his pocket, pulled out a cigarette lighter and flicked it on. Then he backed away a few feet and tossed it toward the vehicle.

THREE

A man's voice penetrated Dean's mind, and he opened his eyes. He pushed himself to his knees and turned his head toward the sound just in time to see a figure clothed in camouflage drop a cigarette lighter to the ground. Immediately, a flame shot up.

Dean jumped to his feet and faced the man behind the flames. "What are you doing?" he yelled.

The man took a step backward, raised his gun and pointed it at Dean. "Harwell? Why are you here?"

Beside him Gwen gasped and coughed from the smoke. The man jerked his attention to her, and that gave Dean the opportunity he needed to find a weapon. A cardiac monitor, jarred from its place on the ambulance wall, lay next to him, and he grabbed it by the handle. With all his strength he heaved the piece of equipment at the man, who sidestepped with a startled cry. Then he turned and ran up the mountainside.

Dean grabbed Gwen's arm and pulled her to her feet. "We've got to get out of here. Right now!"

She looked back at Joe, who was beginning to stir. "I can make it," she said. "Get Joe and the driver out!"

Ignoring her demand, Dean pulled her toward the back door and held her elbow as she scrambled to the ground. She'd taken only a few steps before she stumbled and fell to her knees. Dean wheeled around, grabbed Joe in turn and helped him rise. Together they jumped from the back of the vehicle.

As soon as they were outside, he told Joe, "Get Gwen away from here before the fire reaches the gas tank."

The EMT nodded, pulled her to her feet and half dragged her up the steep slope away from the wreck. Dean could hear her screaming his name as he ran around to the driver's side door. Inside, Wilson was slumped over the wheel. Dean pulled on the handle, but the door refused to open. He tried again, with no success. A glance toward the back of the ambulance told him the fire was spreading underneath. He had to get Wilson out, or they were both going to die in an explosion.

Praying that he could be fast enough, Dean ran to the rear doors and jumped back inside. It took him only a few seconds to find the fire extinguisher, still mounted in its case on the ambulance wall.

Praying that it hadn't been damaged during the wreck, he pulled it free and leaped out. His heart pounded and his hands shook as he remembered the word a trainer at the police academy had taught him: *PASS*, an acronym for *pull, aim, squeeze, sweep*. The temptation was to aim for the fire, but that only made the extinguishing agent fly through the flames without doing any good.

Thanks to his training, it took Dean only a few minutes to extinguish the fire that had spread beneath the ambulance. When he was convinced it was out, he ran back to the driver's door and hammered at the window with the base of the fire extinguisher. After a few blows it shattered, and he reached inside to unlock the door.

Blood was pouring down the side of Wilson's head. Dean placed his fingertips on his neck and was relieved to feel a weak pulse. With the fire out, he debated whether or not to pull Wilson from the cab. Before he could decide, he heard the sounds of sirens and brakes screeching as the first responders came to a stop on the road above.

"Down here," Joe yelled to the firemen and EMTs who jumped from their vehicles and hurried down the embankment toward the wreck.

Dean backed away and let the emergency workers take control of the scene, then walked to where Joe and Gwen stood. Her worried gaze swept over him as he came closer. "Are you okay?" she asked.

He grimaced. "Yeah. How about you?"

"The wound on her head has started to bleed," Joe said. "I'm going to get a new bandage for it."

Dean watched his friend walk away, then turned back to Gwen. She stared at him for a moment before she dropped to her knees and covered her face with her hands, her shoulders shaking with sobs. Unsure what to do, Dean hesitated before he squatted beside her. He started to put his arm around her, but thought better of it. Finally, he braced his hands on his knees and leaned close.

"Gwen, are you all right?" he asked.

She looked up with tear-filled eyes, and his stomach clenched at the memory of how often he'd been the cause of her tears in the past. She had once said she would never forgive him, and he believed her. He wished he could let her know how he regretted everything he had done that had torn their marriage apart, but now was not the time.

She nodded. "When I smelled that gasoline, I was so scared. Then I thought I was the only one who'd survived the wreck." She glanced at the ambulance. The first responders had removed Wilson from inside and were bent over him, administering aid.

Dean smiled. "But you called 911 anyway. That was quick thinking."

Her cheeks flushed and a smile pulled at her lips. "I'm just glad your cell phone fell out of your pocket to make me think of it."

The stilted conversation between the two of them reminded him how different things were now than they'd been years ago. He wished he could go back and tell that young police officer to do things differently, but he couldn't. What was done was done, and the past couldn't be changed.

"Gwen—" he began, but stopped when a familiar voice interrupted him.

"Dean, I was nearly back to town when I got the message to return. What happened?"

He looked up to find his friend the sheriff coming down the embankment. Dean placed a hand on Gwen's elbow and supported her as they rose to their feet. Ben Whitman stopped beside them and glanced from one to the other.

Dean nodded toward the wrecked ambulance. "I guess our guy wasn't through for the day."

Ben frowned and pushed his hat back on his head. "You think the shooter at the trailhead caused this wreck?"

Dean nodded. "Yeah, I saw him." He turned to Gwen. "This is Sheriff Ben Whitman. He's a good friend of mine. You need to tell him your story about what happened by the stream. Then we can fill him in on what went down here." He glanced back at Ben. "This is Gwen."

"It's a pleasure to meet you!" Ben told her. "I've heard a lot about you."

"About me?"

He nodded, a smile curling his lips. "Dean and I have been friends a long time." He glanced at the ring on Dean's hand, and Gwen's mouth dropped open. From her surprised look, Dean guessed she hadn't noticed it before. He wondered how she felt about it.

Her face flushed and she jerked her gaze away. "Then I suppose you know our history."

"Some of it, but right now I'm more interested in what happened when you were attacked. Why don't you tell me about it?"

Dean listened as Gwen recounted her tale of being pursued through the forest by a man wearing a ski mask and how terrified she'd been when he'd leveled the gun and shot at her. When she'd finished, Dean described the shots that had caused the ambulance to go over the side of the mountain and what had happened after that.

"This guy knew me," Dean said. "When I got to my feet, he called me by name. Not long after that, he turned and ran. He'd already started the fire by that time, though."

"Did you recognize his voice?" Ben asked.

Dean shook his head. "No. It was muffled by the ski mask, but there was something familiar about it."

The sheriff sighed. "If you come up with anything that could help us, let me know. Looks like our guy has had a busy day. Instead of a search for just a shooter, now I have to let my deputies know we're looking for a body in the stream, too."

He turned and walked a few feet away before he took out a cell phone. Dean could hear him talking to Dispatch, giving orders to change the focus of the hunt. He'd just finished the call when Joe came to stand beside them.

"How's the driver?" Gwen asked.

A troubled look flashed on Joe's face. "He must have hit his head on the steering wheel when we crashed. He's still unconscious, and we're getting ready to leave with him for the hospital. Sorry, but both of you have to come, too. We want to make sure you don't have any internal injuries."

"And what about you?" Dean asked.

Joe chuckled. "I'll get checked out, too. They're

taking Wilson up to the ambulance right now." He glanced at Gwen. "Miss Anderson, you need to lie down on the stretcher so we can get you up the incline, too."

"I don't need a stretcher," she protested. "I can walk."

Before Joe could answer her, Dean stepped closer. "You've been through a lot this afternoon, Gwen. Joe and the paramedics are just doing their jobs, so do what they say, please."

She opened her mouth as if she meant to argue further, but then closed it and nodded. "Okay, I don't want to be difficult."

Two of the first responders appeared beside them with a stretcher and lowered it for Gwen to lie down. She huffed out another exasperated breath and rolled her eyes before she complied.

Dean couldn't help but chuckle. "I see you haven't changed a bit. You're just as determined and independent as you were when we were married."

Her forehead wrinkled as she studied him. That was the same look she'd given him many times in the past when she was trying to figure out the answer to a burning question. He couldn't help but wonder what she was pondering now.

The EMTs picked up the stretcher and began the trek up the mountainside to the road, where a new ambulance waited. They'd taken only a few steps when Gwen pushed herself up on her elbows and called out to him, "Dean, will I see you at the hospital?"

He raised his hand and waved to her. "You can count on it," he called back.

She took a deep breath and lay back down on the stretcher. "Good."

The word was spoken so softly he wondered if he'd heard her correctly.

Gwen hated him, and he couldn't blame her. He'd come to realize what living with an alcoholic must have been like for her. There was no way he could ever make up for the unhappiness he'd caused her, and no way he would allow her to be hurt more in the future.

She wasn't safe in this mountain community. A killer had tried twice to kill her and would probably try again. She needed to give up the idea of filming a documentary here and put as much distance between herself and this place as possible. Now all Dean had to do was convince her of it.

Gwen sat on the edge of the exam table in the emergency room, her feet dangling over the side and her cell phone pressed to her ear. For the past ten minutes she'd been talking with her mother and explaining what had happened today. To say that her mom was upset was an understatement.

She had always been protective of Gwen, more so than most mothers. Gwen had chalked that up to the fact that she was an only child. Since her divorce from Dean, her mother had made it her mission to try to control Gwen's whole life. Sometimes to the point that Gwen felt she was about to suffocate.

It wasn't the fact she'd twice almost been killed today that had her mother so riled up, though. It was Dean's presence that had unleashed all her mama-bear instincts. "Mom, please," Gwen said for perhaps the tenth time, "there's no need for you to get upset."

"No need?" her mother practically yelled. "That man made you miserable when you were married. He almost destroyed you. As it is, he's turned you into somebody who distrusts every man you meet."

"Mom, let's not go there right now."

"And why not?"

Gwen pulled the phone away from her ear and rolled her eyes in frustration. She'd never yelled at her mother but sometimes felt pushed to the limits. With only a curtain covering the opening into the room, she tried to lower her voice so no one could hear her conversation.

"Because I don't want to talk about that. I just wanted you to know what happened to me today."

She heard her mother's short intake of breath, and then her voice became gentler. "I'm sorry, darling. I'm upset because you were hurt and threatened, but it's more than that. You know what's at stake here."

The guilt she'd carried for the past five years surfaced, and Gwen bit down on her lip. "I know. Don't tell Maggie about this, okay?"

A loud gasp rippled in Gwen's ear. "You don't think I'd tell her that her mother was almost killed, do you? I wouldn't frighten her like that. I love her. And I certainly wouldn't tell her that her mother's now with the father who doesn't even know she exists. Do you have any idea what that would do to a four-year-old child?"

"Of course I do, Mom. You don't have to worry. She's my main concern, and I'll do whatever it takes to protect her."

"Then keep that in mind. No matter what Dean says, don't let him worm his way back into your life. Remember how his drinking almost destroyed you. He'll always be an alcoholic. Don't let him mislead you into believing any differently."

"Mom, please—"

Her mother interrupted before she could finish her sentence. "Let me remind you that when you made the decision not to tell Dean you were pregnant, you said you never intended to see him again. Now you have, and there's no telling what he'll do if he finds out about Maggie."

"I know that, Mom," she whispered.

"Good. Maybe this is the push you need to rethink your relationship with Rick."

Gwen gritted her teeth. "Please don't bring up Rick today. I've told you over and over that we're just good friends. We work together and enjoy going out every once in a while, but that's where it ends."

Her mother sighed. "I know he cares about you, and he's a good man. At least you could give him a chance."

Gwen closed her eyes and rubbed her hand across them. How many times had she had this conversation with her mother? Lately she'd found her resolve slipping, and sometimes it seemed her life would be simpler if she'd just do as her mother asked and try to think of Rick as more than a friend.

"Mom…"

"All I'm asking is that you think about it."

Gwen tightened her grip on the phone and gritted her teeth. "Mom, please, I can't do this now. My head hurts, and I don't want to talk about Rick. We'll talk about it more when I come home."

"You're right," her mother said. "Right now you need to get yourself checked out and make sure you don't have any injuries. You take care of yourself, and I'll take care of Maggie. She's very eager for you to come home. When do you think that will be?"

"As soon as I finish my research. It should be a few more days."

"Let me know, and we'll meet you at the airport."

"I will. And, Mom, thank you for everything you've done for me. I love you."

"You don't have to thank me. Just promise me that you'll think about Maggie's future. She needs a father."

"I know that."

Her mother was silent for a moment before she spoke again. "I hope you know that I only want what's best for you because I love you."

"I love you, too, Mom. I'll talk to you later."

Gwen ended the call and laid the phone beside her on the table, then scrubbed her hands over her face in an effort to relieve the anxiety talking with her mother always provoked. The curtain over the door moved, and Dean called out from the other side, "Gwen, may I come in?"

She glanced back at the phone with wide eyes. How long had he been standing there? Had he heard her speak about Maggie or Rick? She shifted on the table and crossed her arms over her stomach.

"Come in, Dean."

He pulled back the curtain before he stepped into the room. A sad look shadowed his dark eyes, making them stand out in his pale face. His gaze traveled over her before he inhaled. She tried to determine if he had heard her conversation or not, but couldn't tell. He held her gaze for a few seconds before she glanced down.

"I was just talking with my mother."

"And how is she?" he asked.

"She was concerned about what's happened today."

He slipped his hands in his pockets and took a step closer. "I suppose that means she's upset that I'm here with you."

Gwen shook her head. "Dean, please…"

"It's okay, Gwen. I understand how she feels about me, and I don't blame her. But neither you nor your mother have anything to fear from me. All I've ever wanted is for you to be happy. I wouldn't do anything to interfere with that."

She blinked back the tears that filled her eyes and smiled. "I believe you, Dean. No matter what your problems were, you never lied to me."

He took a step closer. "No, I never did, and I'm not going to start now. I've been talking with Ben, and we're both concerned about the attempts on your life today. We think you need to go home while Ben searches for this guy. When he's caught, you can come back and finish your research."

Her eyes widened. "I can't do that. I'm on a schedule to get this project under way. I can't wait while the police look for a murderer they may never find." She shook her head. "No, I'm going to finish my job, and then I'll leave."

"Gwen, listen to me," he said. "You're still in danger. I don't want you to get hurt."

She eased off the table and walked over to face him. "Thank you, but I have a job to do. I'm sure I'll be fine."

He glared at her and raked his hand through his hair. "I'm not going to let you do this."

Her mouth gaped open and she shook her head. "Are you serious? Do you really think you can order me around? We aren't married anymore. I don't have to listen to you."

He couldn't have looked more shocked if she'd slapped him, and she immediately regretted her harsh words. His shoulders sagged and he nodded. "I know I don't have any right to control what you do, especially after what I just overheard."

Panic ripped through her, and it was all she could do not to run for the door. She clasped her hands together and tried to keep them from shaking. "What did you hear?"

He jammed his hands in his pockets again and rocked back on his heels. "I didn't mean to eavesdrop, but I walked up just as you were saying something about a guy named Rick. Are you involved with him?"

She breathed a sigh of relief. If that was all he'd heard, then he still didn't know about Maggie. Gwen nodded. "No. My mother wishes I was, though. He and I work together, and we date some. He's a good man, and I enjoy spending time with him."

Dean's Adam's apple bobbed as he swallowed. "I see," he said. "I realize you have another life now, and I'd like for you to be able to return to it safely." They stared at each other, neither speaking for a few seconds, and then he sighed and rubbed his hand across his eyes. "So, if you won't go home, how about this? Stay at my dude ranch until you're through with your assignment. I'll have one of my employees accompany you to all the locations you want to visit. That way I'll know you're being protected."

She frowned. "You want me to stay at your ranch? I can't do that."

"Why not? I have other guests there. You'll have your own room with a private bath, and you can have as little to do with me as you want. I promise I'll leave you alone."

"I'm not worried about being around you. Our marriage ended years ago, and we both know we can never get back what we once had. I'm just afraid it will be uncomfortable for us."

He smiled. "Then we'll have to make sure to keep things pleasant between us. No rehashing what can't be changed. Just an attempt to be friends. What do you say?"

She thought about it for a moment. It really would make her feel safer if she had someone to accompany her on her research trips. And she had to admit she was curious about the life Dean had made for himself. If she did this, she would have to be careful, though, and guard against letting any word or action give away the secret she'd kept hidden.

Finally, she smiled and nodded. "Thank you, Dean. I'd like to stay at your dude ranch."

A big smile pulled at his lips. "Good. I promise you won't regret it."

Gwen's stomach clenched at his words, and she almost groaned. Something told her Dean was mistaken. She had just made a decision that she might regret for the rest of her life.

FOUR

An hour later Dean stood in the doorway of Gwen's motel room and smiled at the sight of her on her knees, looking under the bed. He tried to push the memory of earlier times like this from his mind, but it was no use. He chuckled, and she glanced up at where he leaned against the doorjamb, his arms crossed.

"Are you sure you have everything?" he asked, a smirk pulling at his lips.

She pushed herself to her feet, brushed her hands against the knees of her jeans and glared at him. "You're not going to bring that up again, are you?"

He smiled and straightened. "I can't help remembering how no matter where we went, you always managed to leave something behind. Do you recall the time you left your makeup case in the bathroom of that St. Louis hotel, and you made me drive two hundred miles back to get it?"

She arched an eyebrow and shrugged. "Only because it was cheaper to pay for the gas to go back than to replace everything that was in that bag."

"So you said." He smiled again. "But I didn't mind."

She started to reply, but the expression on her face suddenly changed to one of uncertainty. With a sigh, she sat down on the bed. Her chin dropped to her chest and she shook her head. "I can't do this, Dean," she said.

He walked over and stared down at her. "Can't do what?"

"I can't go with you if you're going to bring up the past all the time. I've moved on, and I don't want to look back at what we once had."

He nodded and looked at the floor. "I'm sorry. It's just that I thought I'd never see you again, and then all of a sudden you're here and there's a guy pointing a gun at you. In all my years in police work I was never so scared as I was when I woke up on the floor of that ambulance and thought he was going to shoot you."

"I know. I was scared, too."

There was a time when he'd been the one she'd turned to when she was frightened or upset. Then his drinking got bad enough that he became the one who was scaring or upsetting her most of the time. No doubt this Rick guy was the one who comforted her now. The thought left a sour taste in Dean's mouth.

He sighed and rubbed the back of his neck as he eased down to sit beside her. "And I'm sorry for dredging up the past. I guess the news that there's another man in your life was a bit more difficult to take than I thought. But you're correct. I don't have any right to remind you of what used to be. I promised you that I wouldn't do that if you went out to the ranch with me, and I won't." He stood and stretched out his hand as if to help her up, but then thought better of it and curled his fist at his side. "I'll wait for you outside. Come when you're ready."

Without another word he headed toward the door. Once out in the sunshine, he blinked and pulled a pair of sunglasses from his pocket. His mind whirled with a hundred different reasons why he shouldn't take Gwen to his ranch. He wasn't over her—probably never would be—and it would be incredibly painful to see her regularly and know that he wasn't welcome around her anymore. She might say she'd moved on, but she still resented him for how he'd ruined their lives, and he couldn't blame her.

However, there was one overriding reason she should go. Someone had tried twice to kill her, and she'd be safer with Dean than she would be left alone in that motel room.

He turned at the sound of her walking from the room and closing the door behind her. She headed toward her rental car, which one of Ben's deputies had delivered to the hospital. Dean had just stepped over to open the door for her when he heard a man's voice ring out.

"Gwen! Wait!"

They both turned to see a man jogging across the parking lot toward them. The T-shirt and running shorts he wore were wet with perspiration. His sun visor looked drenched, and sweat poured down his face. He grinned as he stopped in front of Gwen, gulped for breath and leaned over with his hands on his knees.

She smiled in welcome. "Mark, how far did you run today?" she asked.

He took a few more breaths before he answered. "I did five miles. I thought you were coming with me this afternoon. I checked before I left, but you weren't in."

Dean's heart did a nosedive into his stomach at the way the man's eyes raked her face, but Gwen only tilted her head to one side, smiled and stared up at him. "I'm sorry. I got involved in scouting locations and was detained."

His forehead wrinkled. "Nothing serious, I hope."

She shook her head. "No." Dean stepped up behind her, and she glanced over her shoulder at him. "Dean," she said, "this is Mark Dyson. He's in the Smokies for a few days." She turned back to Mark. "And this is Dean Harwell, an old friend I ran into today. He owns a dude ranch outside of town, and he's invited me to stay with him for the rest of my visit."

Mark wiped his sweaty hand on his shorts before he stuck it out. "Nice to meet you, Dean."

Dean studied him for a moment before he nodded and shook his hand. "You, too, Mark. So you're a visitor to our mountains, like Gwen?"

He laughed. "Yeah, I guess you could call me that. I live in Knoxville and come here every chance I can. I spend a lot of time hiking the trails around here. I thought Gwen was going to go with me up to Clingman's Dome this afternoon. But when I couldn't find her, I went on a run by myself."

Dean narrowed his eyes a bit and let his gaze travel over Mark, taking in all the details he'd been trained as a police officer to notice. Mark's well-toned body told Dean that this guy must spend a lot of time in the gym. His hands with the manicured fingernails said he didn't do any kind of manual labor, but that wasn't what caught Dean's attention. The indentation on the ring finger of his left hand did. Dean knew what that was from his own experience: Mark was used to wearing a ring. Could it be a wedding ring?

"So, Mark," he said. "You live in Knoxville. Have you lived there long?"

"I got a job offer there when I graduated from college, and I took it. I really like the city and plan on staying."

"College, huh? Where did you graduate?"

Mark fidgeted from one foot to the other and glanced at Gwen before responding. "Harvard Law."

Dean's eyebrows arched. "Wow! That sounds impressive. I don't think I've ever met anyone who graduated from there."

Mark wiped at the sweat that trickled down the side of his face. "It's a great school."

"What kind of law do you practice?"

A slight frown puckered the man's forehead. "Mostly corporate stuff. Too boring to talk about." With a smile, he turned back to Gwen. "So you're checking out of the motel?"

"Yes, but I'm not going home. I'll still be here for a few days."

"Good. Then maybe we can do that climb to Clingman's Dome another day."

"Maybe. It depends on how much work I get done."

He cast a quick glance at Dean, who had inched closer to Gwen. "So, I guess if you're leaving right now, this means we aren't going to have dinner together tonight."

She smiled. "Not tonight. I'm too tired, but you have my cell-phone number. Call me, and we'll see about another night this week."

"I will. I'd like to hear more about that TV special you're working on." He looked back at Dean. "Nice meeting you. Maybe I'll see you again while I'm here."

Dean nodded. "Maybe."

Mark dropped his gaze to his watch and then back at Gwen. "I need to get going, but I'll see you later."

"I'll talk to you soon," Gwen called as he walked away.

When Mark was out of hearing, she spun to face Dean and glared at him. "What was that all about?" she demanded.

"What do you mean?"

"You questioned Mark like he was the suspect in a murder case. It was embarrassing."

"You're overreacting. I just wanted to get a better handle on who he is. He seemed mighty friendly. Have you known him long?"

"No, I met him in the motel lobby the day after I

checked in. Then I ran into him at a restaurant the next night. Since we were both alone, we ended up having dinner together, and he asked me if I'd like to go to Clingman's Dome. You know as much about him as I do, but he seems like a nice man."

His shoulders sagged, and he exhaled a long breath. "I'm not criticizing you. I just want you to be safe. Have you forgotten that you were almost killed today? You need to know someone before you get friendly enough to go for a run or have dinner with him."

She propped her hands on her hips. "And how should I go about getting to know someone better? It seems like having dinner in a public restaurant would be the ideal place to talk and get acquainted."

"Gwen, I was only trying—"

She took a step nearer. "I know what you were trying to do. I've seen you in cop mode before, and you need to stop. I'll remind you once again that we're no longer married, and if this is what it's going to be like with me at your ranch, I can't go."

"You misunderstood me, Gwen. I know we're not married, and I know I'm not a cop anymore. But neither one of those things keeps me from wanting you safe. Please be patient until Ben has a chance to catch whoever this is that tried to kill you today."

She was silent for a moment, and then the anger in her eyes faded. "Okay, but you know this isn't going to be easy. We may try to tell ourselves that we won't dwell on the past, but we can't just forget that we were once married and very much in love."

"I know."

She reached out and grasped his arm. "But we need to put our marriage in perspective. We've been divorced for five years now, and I've built a new life. I don't want my old one to intrude on what I have now."

His heart pricked at her words. He glanced down at her hand and then back to her. "I've always known you'd marry again, but it kind of threw me off guard when I heard you talking to your mother about another guy."

Gwen sucked in her breath and released her hold on him. A look of something close to fear flashed in her eyes, and he frowned. "What else did you hear?" she asked.

"That's all. Was there more? Maybe about how much you love him?"

She breathed what sounded like a sigh of relief and shook her head. "No, I didn't say that."

He struggled to keep from smiling at the satisfaction her words produced in him. He didn't want to think about her married to another man, but he had to finally come to grips with the fact that there really was no going back. She had someone waiting for her in New York, and his life was here now with his grandfather. He took a deep breath and straightened his shoulders. "I want you to be happy. That's all I've ever wanted. I'm sorry I didn't make you happy when we were married."

She blinked to keep tears from flooding her eyes. "Dean, please don't."

He opened his mouth to respond, but his cell phone rang. He pulled it from his pocket and stared at caller ID before he spoke. "Ben, what's up?"

Gwen inched closer. "Is that the sheriff?"

He nodded and frowned as he turned his attention to what his friend was saying. He heard the words, but his mind couldn't accept them. He sagged against the side of her car and covered his eyes with his hand. "No," he muttered over and over.

"Dean, what is it?" she whispered.

He didn't look up at her but continued shaking his head. "I'll be right there," he finally said, then lowered the phone from his ear and slipped it back in his pocket.

After a moment he straightened and lifted his gaze to her. "Gwen," he whispered. He tried to say more, but his voice refused to cooperate.

Gwen stared at him wide-eyed. "Dean, tell me what's happened."

A shudder shook his body, and he closed his eyes for a moment. "They found the body you saw being dumped in the river."

"And you know the person?"

He nodded. "Yes. It was my grandfather."

Gwen wished Dean had let her go with him into the exam room to identify his grandfather's body, but he had insisted he didn't want her to have to experience that. She'd sat for the past few minutes on a bench in the hallway outside the room and waited. She still couldn't believe that James Harwell was dead.

The memory of the first time Dean had brought her to the mountains to meet his grandfather made her smile in spite of her heavy heart. They'd hit it off right away, and Dean had been happy knowing that the man he loved so much approved of the woman he wanted to marry.

For the past five years she'd often thought of Gramps, as she'd called him, and had wanted to get in touch with him. But she couldn't. She didn't want Dean to know where she was or the secret she had hidden from him. Now it was too late for his grandfather to know that he'd left behind a great-granddaughter.

Through the years she'd told herself that by hiding her child from Dean she was protecting Maggie from the horror of having an alcoholic father. In the last days of their marriage, it had been agony for her trying to cope with his constant drinking, his drunken hallucinations and the uncaring attitude about everything in his life. The final decision to leave had come when she'd awakened one night to find him thrashing about in bed from one of his nightmares. When she touched him, he'd attacked her and nearly choked the life from her before she managed to escape.

He'd been repentant the next morning and vowed it would never happen again, but she knew it was a promise he wouldn't be able to keep. In her heart she realized that she couldn't subject the baby she'd just found out she was carrying to a life like that, and she'd left that day. Knowing she had kept Maggie safe had helped to push away the guilt she felt for never telling Dean about his daughter.

Now that she'd seen him again, Gwen couldn't help but wonder if she'd made the right decision by keeping Maggie from Dean and his grandfather. Dean seemed so different, so much closer to the man she'd first fallen in love with, rather than the man who'd frightened her into running away. He'd been sober for four years—four years that Maggie could have had a loving daddy. Gwen shook the thought from her head. What was done couldn't be changed, and there was no need to dwell on it.

The door to the exam room opened, and Dean stepped into the hall. He stopped and stared at her for a moment before he took a hesitant step. She rose as he came toward her. "Are you all right?" she asked.

He nodded. "As much as I can be after seeing the only family I have left lying on a table in the medical examiner's office."

Tears filled her eyes at the pain she saw in his, and her lips quivered. "Ever since I've been here, I half hoped I'd run into him somewhere. I knew he still lived in the same place, but I didn't think he'd want to see me."

"He always loved you, Gwen. In fact, he told me not too long ago that he still prayed for you every day. He said he might not know where you were but that God did, and he prayed that you were safe and happy."

"He was a good man." A tear rolled down her face, and she wiped at it. "I know you'll miss him so much."

Dean nodded, and they sat on the bench where she'd waited. He propped his elbows on his knees and clasped his hands together. He stared down at the floor and shook his head. "I wish you could have seen him at breakfast this morning, Gwen. He had on the Western shirt that was his favorite, and he was so excited about the new colt that had been born last night. Now his lifeless body is in the next room on an exam table."

Gwen closed her eyes for a moment and remembered how scared she'd been when she'd looked down and seen a masked man dumping a body in the river. Now that she knew who it was she was even more troubled. "Dean, evidently the man who tried to kill me is the same one who killed your grandfather. Can you think of anyone who might have a grudge against him or you?"

Dean swallowed and closed his eyes for a moment before he spoke. "I can't think of anybody. I've lived a quiet life since I came back home, and everybody loved my grandfather. He was such a good man, the best I've ever known. He and my grandmother took me in when my parents were killed, as you know. Then after Grandma died he raised me all by himself. The proudest I've ever seen him was when I graduated from college. No one in our family had ever done that. Then when I became a police officer, he couldn't brag enough about me to his friends."

Gwen smiled. "I remember. When he'd come visit us, all he wanted to talk about were the cases you were working on."

A slow smiled pulled at Dean's lips. "Yeah, he kept up with all my cases, even followed the trials I had to testify in. He was always there to support me when things didn't go so well." His face suddenly darkened, and Gwen knew what he was thinking.

"You mean like the Trip King case?" she asked.

Dean exhaled a deep breath. "Yeah. That was one that troubled me more than any of the others."

"Does it still keep you awake at night?"

"Sometimes. I regret how I spiraled into alcoholism after that case." He darted a quick glance at her. "And how it ultimately cost me my marriage. I couldn't have gotten through that time if it hadn't been for Granddad."

She squeezed Dean's hands, then released them. "He did all that because he loved you. Now you need to focus on helping Ben find out who killed him."

"And who tried to kill you, too."

She nodded. "Yes. So concentrate on that. Now tell me what the sheriff said. Does he have any clues to who the killer might be?"

Dean shook his head. "No. They're not even sure what the cause of death was, so they're sending his body to the state lab for an autopsy. It'll be a few days before they get a report on the findings. In the meantime, Ben and his deputies will continue to look for any evidence."

"I doubt you've had time to think about this yet, but what about the funeral?"

He raked his hand through his hair and groaned. "I can't plan anything until his body is returned. I've heard him say many times that he only wanted a graveside service with his closest friends there, but I don't want to even think about that right now."

Gwen reached for Dean's hand again. "Then don't.

We'll wait until the autopsy is completed. Then we'll plan the funeral."

His breath hitched in his throat, and he stared at her in disbelief. "*We'll* plan the funeral? Do you mean you'll stay and help me get through it?"

"Of course I will. I loved him, and I don't want you to have to face this alone."

Dean's eyes softened, and his Adam's apple bobbed as he swallowed. "Thank you, Gwen. I really appreciate that." He took a deep breath. "Then let's get going. We need to get you settled and see if Shorty has anything left from supper."

"Shorty? Is he still there?"

Dean smiled. "Yeah, I don't think he'll ever leave. He's like family, and he's also the best cook in these mountains. I don't know what we would do without him."

The memory of earlier times at the Harwell ranch returned, and she again felt the sting of tears. She could almost see Gramps, a tranquil expression on his face, sitting in front of the big fireplace in the den with a cup of coffee after finishing one of Shorty's big meals, and talking about how God had blessed him. "I have a wonderful grandson, his beautiful wife and the best friends a man could ever have," he would say, and they would all smile and drink their coffee as they sat snug in the mountain home where Dean had grown up.

It was memories like that, coupled with the secret that was weighing on her mind, that made Gwen wonder if she was going to be able to go back to Little Pigeon Ranch. She took a deep breath and smiled.

"I remember Shorty. If you'd told me he was still the cook, I wouldn't have had any trouble deciding to go with you. Now I'm starving."

They stood to leave, but Dean caught her arm to stop her. She turned and looked at him, and her heart pricked at the sad expression on his face. "Gwen, I can't tell you how many times I've wanted to bring you back to the ranch and let you see what my life has become there, but I never would have wanted it to be this way."

She nodded and grasped his arm once more. "Don't think about that, Dean. Let's just focus on catching whoever killed Gramps."

He sucked in his breath and shook his head. "I'm not a police officer anymore. I gave that up years ago."

"You may not be a police officer, but you're still the grandson he was so proud of. You owe it to him to help Ben find his killer. I know you can do it."

The lost look in Dean's eyes turned to one of uncertainty as he stared at her. "I don't know whether I can or not. I'm not the same person you knew years ago."

"No, you're not. I can tell that just in the time I've been around you today. I'm beginning to see that you're a better man than you were then. I want to help you any way I can. Just tell me how."

He looked down at her hand on his arm and then back up at her face. "Just stay with me until we catch this guy. Then you can go home and put me out of your mind."

She heard the silent plea in his voice and knew he needed someone by his side during this time. But she also had a daughter who needed her, and she didn't know how long she could be away from Maggie. Gwen squeezed his hand. "Dean, you may never find out who did this, so I don't think I should promise I'll stay until that happens. But I will stay until we can bury Gramps together."

A sigh of relief rippled from his mouth. "Thank you, Gwen. I can't tell you how much that means to me."

Then he took her by the arm and guided her down the hallway toward the parking lot. The pressure his fingers exerted made her skin grow warm—a reminder of how deeply she'd loved him at one time. The thought scared her, and she gently pulled free. She had to be careful, not let her guard down, if she was to keep the secret she didn't dare tell him.

The truth that he had a daughter he'd never known could destroy him and send him spiraling back into the life of alcoholism he'd worked so hard to overcome. Not only that, but he would hate Gwen forever if he learned the truth, and she didn't think she could stand that.

FIVE

Dean had always felt his spirits lift when he turned onto the winding road toward the rambling log house where he'd grown up. Today things were different, however. Ben had called ahead, and all the ranch hands, their cowboy hats over their hearts, stood in the front yard in silence along with the guests. They watched as he pulled the car to a stop.

He turned off the engine and sat staring at the house for a moment, unable to move. The flag that always waved on a pole in the front yard had been lowered to half-staff, and his grandfather's rocking chair, his favorite place to be in the early evening, stood empty on the front porch. Dean fought back the tears stinging his eyes.

Beside him Gwen looked out the window and gave his hand a quick squeeze. "It hasn't changed a bit," she said. "There's something about this house that made me feel welcome the first time I saw it, and it feels the same now."

Dean rubbed his hands over his eyes and nodded. "That was Granddad—he was the one who made this place feel so welcoming. It doesn't seem right to come home and not have him here." He took a deep breath. "Well, I need to thank everybody for waiting out here."

He opened the door and climbed out. Gwen met him in front of the car and they walked toward those gathered in the front yard. His foreman was the first to meet him. His face lined with grief, Emmett grasped his Stetson in his left hand and extended his right to Dean.

Dean blinked back the tears and grasped it tightly. The memory returned of how Emmett had looked the first time he'd seen him—a rugged cowboy standing in the front yard to welcome Dean when his grandparents brought him home after his parents were killed. During those dark days, as he was trying to come to grips with the fact that his mother and father were never coming back, Emmett had been there for him.

"I'm sorry about James," the foreman said. "He was a good man. I want you to know I'll do anything I can to help you during this time. Just call on me, and I'll be ready."

"I know you will. You've been a loyal employee here ever since I can remember, but you're really like family."

Emmett's eyes sparkled with unshed tears as he turned to Gwen and smiled. "It's good to see you again, Miss Gwen. We've missed you around here."

She smiled and gave Emmett a quick hug. "Thank

you. I've thought of you often since I was last here. It's good to see you again."

Emmett ducked his head and nodded as he stepped back into the group of employees. Dean moved next to Shorty, whose eyelids were red and swollen, and pulled him into a bear hug.

"I'm sorry, Dean," the wiry little cook said, his chin trembling. "I don't know how we're gonna make it around here without him."

Dean nodded and patted his back before relaxing his hold. "The two of you have been together for a long time."

Shorty wiped at his eyes. "About twenty years now. I came to work here right after your grandmother died, and it's been my home ever since."

"And it still is, Shorty. That won't ever change."

Gwen stepped up beside him, and Shorty's eyes grew wide. "Miss Gwen? I'd 'bout given up that we'd ever see you again. Welcome home."

Gwen stiffened for just a moment before she smiled and gave him a hug. "Hello, Shorty. It's good to see you, but I'm sorry it's under these circumstances."

His mouth hung open and he struggled to speak. "B-but what are you doing here?"

"It's a long story, and I'll tell you all about it later." She glanced at Dean. "But for now, do you have anything left to eat? We're starved."

The cook grinned and wiped his eyes once more before he turned and started up the steps to the front porch. He peered over his shoulder from Dean to

Gwen. "There's always something to eat in my kitchen. Come on in, and I'll get it ready."

When he'd gone into the house Dean turned to face the group assembled in the front yard. He cleared his throat and let his gaze drift over them. "I want to thank all of you for being here. This is a hard time for me, and it's going to get a lot harder to face the fact that my grandfather is gone." He paused and took a shaky breath. "But I want all our guests to know that we still intend to give you the full experience of visiting a dude ranch in the mountains. Shorty will be serving breakfast in the main dining room tomorrow morning from seven until nine as usual, and all trail rides and hiking trips that you've signed up for will be leaving as scheduled. My grandfather would want you to enjoy your vacation, and we're going to see that you do. Some of our employees will be patrolling the grounds around the clock to see that you remain safe. So go on with your plans for the evening, and I'll see you all tomorrow."

One by one the guests stepped up to Dean, shook his hand and murmured their condolences. Then they began to drift away, some to rooms inside the main house and others to cabins scattered over the rolling landscape.

When they'd all left, Dean turned back to the ranch hands, who were still standing in the yard. They all seemed to be staring at Gwen as if trying to decide what she was doing with him. He decided against telling them that she was his ex-wife.

"Thanks for being here," he said instead. "I know

you're all probably wondering who this lovely lady is. She's Gwen Anderson, a friend of mine. She's here to scout locations for a documentary her TV network will begin filming soon and will be staying with us for a few days."

A tall, lanky cowboy stuck out his hand and smiled. "My name's Luke, ma'am. It's good to meet you. I was with Dean on the trail ride when we saw you shot. I'm glad you weren't hurt."

She took his hand and shook it. "It's good to meet you, Luke. I'm sorry I don't remember seeing you at the parking lot, but you probably understand why."

"If there's anything you need while you're staying with us, let me know. I'll be glad to help you in any way I can. And so will any of our employees."

"Thank you. I appreciate that."

Luke turned his attention back to Dean. "Don't worry about anything. We'll make sure everything keeps running like James would want. Is there anything I can do for you right now?"

Dean glanced over the cowboys who worked so hard to help his grandfather and him make the ranch a place guests would want to come visit again. His throat closed up at the thought of how his granddad had valued each one of them. "No. Granddad always said he was blessed with the best workers of any of the dude ranches in the mountains. So I guess it's time for us all to get back to work and make sure that everything is just like he'd want it for tomorrow."

"I'll talk to you later, Dean," Emmett said as he stepped up next to Luke and motioned for the men to leave. Some headed toward the horse barn in the field behind the house to finish night chores, while others walked toward the bunkhouse about two hundred yards away.

As they drifted off, Dean caught a glimpse of Billy Champion, a neighbor who had become a good friend of his grandfather's over the past year, standing at the back of the crowd, his hands in his pockets and his head bowed.

"Billy," Dean called out. "I didn't see you there."

The man raised his head, and Dean sucked in his breath at the tortured look on his face. Slowly he walked toward them, his eyes glued to Dean's. "Emmett called me when he got the news, and I came right over. I still can't believe it's true. How could this have happened?"

Dean shook his head. "I don't know. I'm still trying to believe it myself." Next to him Gwen stirred, and he glanced at her. "I'm sorry, Billy. I guess you heard me introduce Gwen. She's a TV producer from New York who's in the mountains for a few days. Gwen, this is Billy Champion. He's one of Granddad's closest friends. He rents a cabin on the back side of the ranch and works at Lambert's Practice Arena."

"You mean the one we went to that time when you were going to show me your calf roping skills?"

Dean blushed and nodded. "Yeah, as I remember that didn't turn out too well. Billy helps Mr. Lambert handle the bucking stock—broncs and bulls. He knows everything there is to know about livestock."

"Oh," Gwen said with a shiver. "I've seen some

of those rodeo events on television, and they really look dangerous."

Billy smiled. "They can be, and the stock can be, too, because they all have different personalities. That's why after spending a day over there I enjoy coming here and beating Dean or James at chess."

"And that's not an easy thing to do, either," Gwen said as she held her hand out. "I'm glad to meet you, Billy."

He smiled and shook it, then tilted his head to one side and stared at her, his eyebrows wrinkled in a frown. "Gwen?" he said. "You look so familiar. It's almost like…" Before he could finish his thought, he snapped his fingers and glanced at Dean. "I know why she's so familiar. James showed me a picture of her once when I was here. It was your wedding photo, Dean." He turned back to Gwen. "You aren't just a friend. You're his ex-wife."

Dean spoke up before she could answer. "Yes, I'm sure Granddad told you we're divorced. Have been for five years now."

"Yeah, that's what he said." Billy stared at Gwen a moment longer before he turned back to Dean. "I didn't mean to stick my nose in your business. It was just such a shock to remember where I'd seen her."

"That's okay. Granddad always loved Gwen. He talked about her a lot."

"I could tell he cared a lot about her." Billy took a deep breath and looked down at his watch. "It's getting late, and I have to make sure my horse is taken care of for the night. I'd better be getting on home. Let me know if I can do anything for you."

"I will," Dean said. He and Gwen watched Billy walk over to a dust-covered Jeep that sat at the edge of the front yard. When he'd driven away, Dean held out his hand toward the front door. "Ready to get something to eat?"

As Gwen climbed the steps to the front porch, he felt a tingle of pleasure in the knowledge that she was here with him after all these years. And she'd agreed to help him with the funeral. Despite the support he knew he'd get from his friends and the community, it meant so much to have her by his side for all this.

A small voice in his head cautioned him to be careful, though. Gwen agreed to come here only because someone had tried to kill her and because she knew how difficult the next few days were going to be for him.

She might have agreed to stay temporarily, but he'd seen the truth in her eyes. The thought that she didn't want to be here and didn't want to be around him felt like a knife slicing through his heart. As soon as she could complete her work, she'd be on a plane back to New York, and he'd be more lonely than ever.

With heavy footsteps he trudged up to the porch and reached out to open the door, then hesitated, halted by the sudden feeling of loss that radiated through his body. His grandfather wasn't inside the house he loved, and he was never coming back. Gwen didn't intend to stay, either, and the thought felt like an anvil crushing Dean's chest.

In the old days two problems like that would have had him reaching for a bottle of liquor, but he couldn't do that now. He'd come too far and overcome too much to let himself be pulled back into his old lifestyle.

Besides, he wanted to show Gwen how he'd changed. Maybe if he could do that she'd agree to let him see her every once in a while. Not on a regular basis, of course, but just enough to satisfy the hunger in his heart for her. And just enough to gain forgiveness from the only woman he'd ever loved.

The inside of the house had changed somewhat in the years since Gwen had been away. The last time she'd been here, Gramps was just beginning to turn his farm into a dude ranch. Now there were indications everywhere that it had become a lucrative venture.

As they stepped into the great room, where she'd spent many happy hours with Dean and his grandfather, she saw that the big fireplace still was the focal point, but a big television hung above it now and comfortable couches and chairs were scattered about. In one corner was a table with brochures on it advertising sights to see and adventures to experience in the Smokies. A table on the opposite wall held machines for making coffee and tea and large baskets of packaged snacks. The whole room seemed to have been specially designed for the comfort of guests.

Off to the left of the great room she stared at what had once been a small office with a desk for keeping farm records. Now it contained filing cabinets and a computer workstation that could rival her office equipment at the television station in New York.

She'd never thought she'd see this place again, but now she was here. And she found that it felt so right. She quickly dismissed that thought from her mind.

Nothing about this was right. She and Dean were divorced, and she would be leaving as soon as she'd finished helping him plan the funeral for his grandfather. In the meantime, there were still locations to be scouted, and she intended to get that job done right away so she could be free to help with the planning when Gramps's body was returned. Then she could get back to New York, where she belonged.

She stepped into the dining room behind Dean and stared in amazement at how the room had changed. "It's so much bigger," she said in disbelief.

He chuckled. "The space we had wasn't big enough to accommodate the number of guests we wanted, so we knocked out the back wall and enlarged it."

Gwen let her gaze drift over the room. Two long rustic wooden tables with benches stood in the center of the room, and smaller tables were scattered around the walls. She turned to Dean and shook her head in amazement. "I never dreamed you would have this many guests. How many do you usually accommodate at one time?"

He shrugged. "That depends on how many people are staying in the cabins. We have twelve on the ranch and some sleep as many as eight people. Then we have a few guest rooms here in the main house. Business has been good for the past few years, though, and we stay fully booked most of the time."

She came to a halt and stared at him. "Are all your rooms in the main house occupied with guests right now?"

"Yeah. I think we're at capacity."

She narrowed her eyes and propped her hands on her hips. "So where did you think you'd put me when you talked me into coming home with you?"

"I thought I'd give you my room, and I would sleep in the bunkhouse with the ranch hands." His eyes darkened and he swallowed. "But I guess I won't have to do that now. I can put you in Granddad's room."

Her heart pricked at the sorrow on his face, and she reached for his hand. "Are you sure about this, Dean? If it's going to cause you any stress to think about your grandfather's room being occupied by someone else, I can go back to the motel."

His gaze traveled over her, and her breath hitched in her throat. It was almost as if he was caressing her with his eyes. After a moment he pulled his hand free from hers. "The only thing that's giving me comfort right now is the fact that you're here with me. I don't want to face this alone, and I don't want you in further danger. So for the time being, let's make the best of a bad situation."

She was about to respond when the door to the kitchen burst open and Shorty barreled into the room. He grinned and held up two plates. "Here's that supper I saved you from the cookout—chuckwagon steak, baked beans and my famous sourdough bread. Hot and ready to eat."

Gwen's stomach growled as the scent of the food tickled her nose. She closed her eyes and sniffed. "Oh, that smells delicious. I haven't had sourdough bread since my last visit here."

Shorty set the plates on one of the tables at the side of the room and wiped his hands on the long white apron he wore. "Well, missy, while you're here, I'll make sure you have enough to satisfy your appetite."

Gwen laughed and walked to the table. She was about to pull out the chair to sit when she felt Dean at her back. Before she could move, he'd pulled the chair back from the table and held it for her.

She looked up at him and then dropped her gaze at the intense expression on his face. Without saying anything, she eased down into the chair. She could feel his hands against her back as he pushed the chair closer to the table, and a tingle of pleasure rippled through her body.

His hand brushed against her shoulder, and his breath fanned the side of her face as he leaned closer. "Welcome back to Little Pigeon Ranch, Gwen. I hope you'll enjoy your stay with us and that we can repair some of the hurt we've caused each other."

His voice held a pleading quality, and she glanced up at him. "I hope so, too, Dean."

He smiled and walked around to the chair facing her. "Then there's no better way to get started than to sit down to one of Shorty's meals."

Before she could answer, the cook pushed the kitchen

door open and stuck his head back in. "Let me know if you need seconds, but save some room. I have peach cobbler for dessert."

Gwen laughed as she picked up her fork and knife. "I can see I'm going to have to watch it while I'm here. I'm not used to eating like this, but I know the food will be too good for me to resist."

Shorty grinned and ducked back in the kitchen. She cut into her steak and put the first bite in her mouth. Her eyes closed, and she gave a groan of satisfaction. "Delicious. I haven't had anything this good in a long time."

Dean looked up from cutting his own meat and smiled. "Really? You were always a good cook. What do folks up in New York eat?"

She swallowed the food in her mouth and laughed as she cut into the steak again. "Macaroni and cheese is one of the favorites at my house."

The words were barely out of her mouth before she realized what she'd said. That was Maggie's favorite dish, and she begged for it several times a week. Gwen's hand froze on her knife, and she cast a wild-eyed look at Dean.

A small frown wrinkled his forehead, and he studied her with interest. "Since when did you start eating macaroni and cheese? You never used to like it."

"Uh, I—I like quick and easy-to-fix dishes these days." Her face grew warm, and she stuffed another bite into her mouth and chewed.

Dean grinned briefly. "I can't argue with that."

For the next few minutes they concentrated on

their meal without speaking. By the time Gwen had cleaned her plate, her pulse had quit pounding at the thought of how close she'd come to revealing more than she should. She took a sip from her coffee cup and watched as Dean scraped up the last bite of his peach cobbler.

She leaned back in her chair and sighed. "That was delicious. I haven't had a meal like that in ages."

Before Dean could answer, Shorty walked out of the kitchen and stopped at their table. "I put a tray with a fresh pot of coffee and some cups on the front porch. It's a nice night, and the sky is full of stars. Go out there and relax. It's been a rough day."

"Let me help you," Gwen said as she rose and started to stack the dishes.

Shorty shook his head and took the plate she held from her hand. "I've got this. You go on and keep Dean company. I'll clean up the kitchen. Then I'll head out to the bunkhouse. I have to be up early to cook breakfast."

Dean pushed back from the table and stood. "Thanks, Shorty. I'll see you in the morning."

"Good night, Shorty. It's wonderful seeing you again," Gwen said and turned toward the door.

She was almost to it when she heard the cook's voice. "It's good seeing you, too, Miss Gwen. It just ain't been the same around here since you quit coming. It's good to have you back."

She felt her face grow warm, but didn't turn and look at him as she headed out of the dining room, Dean right behind her. When she stepped onto the porch, she walked to the railing, braced her arms on it and stared up at the stars. Dean stopped beside her and directed his gaze to the sky also.

"I've never seen the stars so bright," she said. "They look like jewels twinkling in the sky."

His shoulder brushed hers as he leaned forward. "They're always brighter here in the mountains. Since we're not in town, they don't have to compete with the streetlights and the harsh glare of all the neon signs. Then when the sky's clear like tonight, it makes the heavens really light up." He lifted his arm and pointed. "Look at the stars in the Big Dipper. We might not be able to see them if we were looking at them in a city."

His voice held a note of reverence, and it reminded her of the young man he'd been when they'd first met. He wasn't jaded by his job then, and he had enjoyed living his life to the fullest.

"You're happy here, aren't you, Dean?" she murmured.

He nodded but didn't take his eyes off the sky. "I found myself again here. I came to understand how much God loved me, and I completely turned my life over to Him." Dean darted a quick glance at her and then back to the stars. "I only wish I'd found Him sooner. If I had, maybe I could have saved our marriage. But I didn't, and all I can do now is move forward."

She didn't say anything for a moment. "I'm glad I got to see how happy you are. I can go back to New York knowing that you're all right."

He straightened and turned to her. "When you go

back, do you think we might be able to stay in touch? Maybe just talk on the phone every once in a while? Or maybe I could come to New York and spend a weekend sometime. I've never been there, and you could show me the sights."

Panic rushed through her, and she grasped the railing tighter to keep him from seeing how her hands were trembling. She bit down on her lip and closed her eyes for a brief moment before she took a deep breath and turned to him.

"Don't do this, Dean."

"Don't do what?" he asked.

"I know seeing me today has been a shock to you, and I'm thankful you were there to save my life. But you need to understand that whatever we had is over. Our marriage ended five years ago, and it's impossible to change that. You have your life here, and I have mine in New York."

He swallowed and stared into her eyes. "I'm sorry, Gwen. I won't do anything to make you uncomfortable again."

"Thank you."

He pursed his lips and sighed as he glanced at the coffeepot on the table. "I guess the coffee's cold by now. I'll take it inside. It's time I was getting to bed anyway. We get up early around here in the morning, and I have a lot to do tomorrow."

She nodded. "I'm sure you do, and I don't want to be in your way. If you have an extra horse that isn't going on a trail ride tomorrow, I'd like to borrow it. I remember a beautiful waterfall in the mountains back of the ranch. I'd like to ride up there and see if there are any spots that would be good locations for us to use."

"I'll see that you have a horse, but I don't think it's a good idea for you to go alone. I'll get one of the staff to ride along with you."

"You don't have to do that."

He picked up the tray holding the coffeepot and cups and stared at her. "You were nearly killed twice today. Please don't fight me on this. I'm only thinking of your safety."

She hesitated for a moment, then nodded. "Okay. I have to confess I'd feel better having someone along."

"Good. Now follow me, and I'll show you to your room. Shorty told me he'd made it up for you while we were eating supper."

"I'll be right there," she said, then turned back around to look up at the stars.

Tears pooled in her eyes as Dean walked into the house. She'd never felt so guilty as she did right now. Dean didn't deserve what she was doing by keeping his daughter a secret from him. But how could she tell him?

Even with the horrible events of the day, being with him had been the happiest she'd felt in a long time. Earlier he had looked at her with such hope that maybe they could heal the past, but she couldn't let that happen. Maybe she was being selfish, but she didn't think she could stand to see his gentle look turn to one of hatred toward her.

She wiped at the tears in her eyes and straightened her shoulders. She'd made her decision and now had to live with it. The best thing for her to do right now was finish her location project and get out of the Smokies as fast as she could.

SIX

Dean was finishing his second cup of coffee the next morning when Gwen entered the dining room. He rose from his chair and studied her as she walked toward him. To look at her no one would suspect that she had almost been killed twice the day before. Her eyes sparkled this morning after getting a good night's sleep, and from the pink flush of her cheeks he thought the fresh mountain air must be agreeing with her.

She smiled as she came toward him in the deserted room, and a pang of regret thudded in his heart. Having her here was the best thing that could have happened to him at this time, but he knew she'd soon be gone. He had to make sure he did nothing to make her uncomfortable. That didn't mean, however, he wasn't going to keep trying to convince her to stay in touch after she returned to New York.

He held her chair as she smiled up at him and slipped into it. "Where are all the guests?" she asked.

"Out enjoying a day in the mountains. Breakfast is over at nine o'clock around here."

She stared down at her watch. "I guess I slept in longer than I meant to." She arched an eyebrow and directed her gaze to his cup of coffee. "It looks like somebody is still hanging around, though."

He chuckled and took another sip. "I was waiting for you. Shorty said to let him know when you were ready to eat. He has pancakes and bacon for you."

The kitchen door opened, and Shorty bustled into the room with a coffeepot. "And I have them cooking right now. I brought you a cup of coffee to get you started."

Gwen looked up at him and smiled. "Thanks, Shorty. I hope my tardiness hasn't caused you any problems this morning, but I just couldn't get out of bed."

He grinned. "Not a bit. You deserved to sleep late after the day you had yesterday. I couldn't believe it when Dean told me what happened. I'm just thankful you're alive and that you've come back to visit us."

"Well, I'm certainly enjoying being here, and your cooking has to be one of the highlights. I imagine that's what keeps the guests coming back."

Shorty's chest puffed out with pride as he shook his head. "Aw, I don't know 'bout that. Dean does a mighty good job of running this place. For the past two years James has been sick, and Dean handled everything by himself."

Gwen looked at Dean and frowned. "You never told me Gramps was sick. What was the matter with him?"

"He was diagnosed with cancer and went through

chemo and radiation. For the past six months he's been better. We thought he might have licked the disease and was going to make it." Dean paused and bit his lip. "Of course, we never figured on somebody wanting to kill him."

"I'd better get those pancakes," Shorty said as he sniffed and turned away. "Be back in a few minutes."

When he'd stepped into the kitchen, Gwen reached across the table and covered Dean's hand with hers. "I'm so sorry I didn't know he was sick."

The touch of her hand made his skin grow warm, and he pulled free of her grasp. "How could you have known? We had no idea where you were."

She sat back in her chair and stared at him. "Did you really not know? I mean, after all, this is the twenty-first century, and you can usually find anybody on the internet if you look hard enough."

"I know that."

Her face paled a bit, and he frowned at her reaction. She swallowed before she spoke. "Then did you ever try to find me?"

He sighed and shook his head. "The day I signed the divorce papers I promised you I would never look for you, and I haven't. I wanted to." A harsh chuckle rumbled in his throat. "You have no idea how badly I wanted to find you, but I promised you I wouldn't. And now here you are, without any help from me. Don't you think that's strange?"

She took a sip of her coffee and shrugged. "Not strange. Just a coincidence. If it wasn't for my work assignment, I wouldn't be. I certainly didn't expect to see you here."

He tilted his head to one side and smiled. "I prefer to think that God brought you here for a reason. Maybe for us to know each other again."

She started to respond, but Shorty came back in with her pancakes just then and set them in front of her. He wiped his hands on his long apron and looked down at Dean. "If you don't need me this morning, I got some personal business I gotta take care of. All the guests will be out until late this afternoon." He turned his attention to Gwen. "Most of our guests are either out sightseeing or on trail rides during the day, so we don't have lunch here. There's sandwich fixings in the kitchen for you, though. I'll be back in plenty of time to get supper ready."

"Don't worry about me," Gwen said. "I can fend for myself."

"I think everything's under control," Dean said to Shorty. "Go on and do whatever you have to do, and I'll see you at supper."

Shorty nodded and turned back to the kitchen. When he'd closed the door behind him, Gwen leaned forward and glared at her ex. "As I was about to say before we were interrupted, don't go reading more into my presence here than what it is. God didn't bring me back. My network sent me here, and that's the only reason. And as soon as I eat breakfast I need to get to work. Did you check to see if there's a horse I can borrow?"

He didn't speak for a moment, just stared at her.

Then he sighed and picked up his coffee cup. "Princess is available. She's a gentle mare that's good for people not used to riding, and it's an easy trip up to Crystal Falls. Emmett's going to go with you in case you have any problems. I don't imagine you get much time to ride in the city."

"You're wrong," she said. "Rick has a stable of horses at his house in the Hamptons. We ride there quite often."

Dean's mouth dropped open, and he sat back in his chair. "Wow! A house in the Hamptons. He sounds like quite a catch. Your first husband could never have given you anything like that on a cop's salary."

Her face grew warm at the sarcastic tone of his voice, and she gritted her teeth. Before she could say anything, her cell phone rang, and she angrily pulled it from her pocket. "Hello," she snarled.

Her features immediately softened, and she smiled. "Good morning to you, too. How are you today?"

Dean picked up a fork and began to trace patterns on the tablecloth with the tines. He had no idea who was on the phone, but she seemed happy to hear from whoever it was.

"Oh, I can't," she said. "I'm going to scout out some locations up around Crystal Falls this morning."

She paused a moment. "You know the place? That doesn't surprise me. You seem to know most of the trails around here. Would you like to come with me?" She listened for a moment before she spoke again. "I see. Then, yes, I'd love to have dinner with you. See you at seven. Enjoy your day in the Smokies. 'Bye."

She ended the call, and Dean leaned forward and crossed his arms on the table. "Who was that?"

"Mark Dyson."

Dean's forehead wrinkled. "The guy I met at the motel yesterday? Are you having dinner with him tonight?"

"Yes. He has to leave tomorrow and wanted to see me again before then."

"Tell me once more how you met this guy?"

She rolled her eyes and huffed out a long breath. "Honestly, Dean, you act like you have a right to check into my life, and you don't. I can see whoever I want without your approval."

The muscle in his jaw flexed, and he glared at her. "I know that. You've certainly reminded me of it often enough since you've been here, but I'm just trying to protect you. Somebody tried to kill you, and everybody around you is a suspect. Now, what do you know about Mark Dyson?"

She crossed her arms and glared back. "He's a lawyer in Knoxville, and he seems like a nice man. That's all I know."

"You ran into him in the motel office, you said. How did he happen to strike up a conversation with you?"

"I don't know. I bumped into him when I turned around from asking the desk clerk a question, and he was very apologetic. He insisted on buying me a cup of coffee for being so clumsy, and we just got to talking. He's a very interesting person."

"What did you talk about?"

"When I told him I was a TV producer here to scout locations for a documentary, he was very interested. It seems he watches a lot of documentaries, and he thought the subject of ours would be very successful."

Dean let her words sink in for a moment. Something didn't seem right here, but he couldn't put his finger on what it was. "You told me you were doing a documentary about the Smokies. I thought the subject was the beauty of the scenery and the wildlife in the mountains. Is that right?"

She nodded. "Well, yes, but it's really about what's happening to the environment."

"What do you mean?"

"We're trying to alert the public to how the Earth's environment is being destroyed, and the Smokies is just one part of it. We also are going to have footage from the rain forest."

"So this isn't just a travel documentary. It's a report on how our lifestyles are affecting our surroundings."

"That's right. You live in these mountains. You surely can see the effect air pollution is having on the trees and wildlife. The Environmental Protection Agency is trying to reduce pollution by having fossil fuel–burning power plants cut down on harmful emissions and factories from illegally dumping waste into water sources. We're going to show some of the companies that are under investigation right now for causing the most harm."

He frowned. "That sounds like an issue that may

have a lot of controversy connected to it. Are you planning to reveal the names of those involved?"

She nodded. "Yes. One of them is located near here—the North Fork Chemical Company. It's owned by a group of investors from all over the country."

"Yeah, I've heard of that one. But, Gwen, I don't know. This sounds—"

She glanced at her watch and jumped to her feet. "It's getting late, and I don't have time to talk about this now. I need to get going. Do you think Emmett is ready to go with me?"

"I told him I'd call him on the intercom when you were heading to the barn."

"You have an intercom that's connected to the barn?"

"It's a safety feature. We had smoke detectors installed there about two years ago. Since the house is so far away, we wanted to make sure we could hear the alarm."

"That seems like a wise thing to do."

Dean pushed back from the table and stood. "I'd go with you today, but I have some work to do in the office. I'll go let Emmett know you're on your way."

"Thanks, Dean. I'll see you this afternoon sometime."

With that, she turned and dashed from the room. As Dean watched her go, he found his thoughts returning to Mark Dyson. Something about the guy didn't ring true, but Dean didn't know what it was. Being a cop had taught him that when he had misgivings about someone or something, he needed to check it out, and he knew just what to do. Gwen was right. You could find everything on the internet.

He strode from the dining room, entered the office and flipped on the intercom. After informing Emmett that Gwen was on her way, he sat down at the computer and within seconds was surfing the internet, looking for anything he could find out about Mark Dyson. His name and law firm came up, and Dean read all the information on the website. It looked like any other site for anyone seeking legal assistance.

He sat back in his chair for a moment, then typed "Mark Dyson litigation" into the search engine. His eyes grew wide as several articles appeared, relating the latest cases he'd handled. Dean read for several minutes before he turned off the computer and slumped in his seat.

He'd been right to worry but didn't have enough information yet to know what was going on. He knew one thing, however. He had to tell Gwen right away that Mark Dyson was one of the lead attorneys representing North Fork Chemical Company in a current class-action lawsuit filed against them.

It couldn't be a coincidence that Mark had bumped into Gwen right when she was about to produce a documentary revealing his client's problems to the world. But what did he hope to learn by appearing to befriend Gwen? Whatever it was, Dean wasn't about to ignore the suspicion he had about Mark's motives. There had to be an agenda of some kind, and Dean intended to find out what it was.

* * *

Gwen strode toward the barn and tried to focus on what she wanted to accomplish for the day. She needed to finish up her location shots so she could get out of here. The tension between Dean and herself seemed to be escalating the longer they were around each other. She'd almost slipped and mentioned Maggie several times since she'd been here, and now Dean was acting like a jealous suitor, making sarcastic remarks about Rick and being suspicious of Mark.

She needed to leave, and the sooner the better. She'd take her pictures today, and then...

Her eyes grew wide, and she stopped in the middle of the path that led to the barn. With a loud thump, she slapped the palm of her hand against her forehead. How was she going to take any pictures? The man who'd tried to kill her yesterday had taken her camera.

Then she remembered the cell phone in her pocket and pulled it out. She could take as many pictures as she liked and email them to her office in New York. Sure, the quality wouldn't be as high as with her usual camera, but this was just a scouting trip; professional-quality shots could come later. Problem solved. With a smile on her face, she pumped her fist in the air and continued toward the barn.

The corral adjacent to the barn held only two horses this morning, the others probably out on a trail ride. She wondered if one of the pair could be Princess as she walked over to the fence and stopped to gaze at the two sleek mares. Both looked docile enough that she was sure she could handle either one.

She turned and walked toward the entrance of the barn, but stopped a few paces outside when a large tan-and-white collie emerged. The dog stopped and stared at her with dark, almond-shaped eyes. From the looks of her Gwen knew right away this had to be a new mother, and from the look of her belly she must have just finished nursing her puppies.

Gwen squatted down and held out her hand. "Hello, girl. Do you have some babies around here?"

The collie inched closer and sniffed at her fingers, then licked them. Gwen smiled and reached out tentatively to touch the dog's flat head. When she heard a soft whine, she let her hand drift over the ears, with tips that folded forward. "You're the most beautiful dog I've ever seen."

"I see you've met Sadie."

Gwen jerked her head up and smiled as Emmett stepped out of the barn. He stopped beside her, and she gave the dog one last pat before she rose to her feet. "She's a beauty. Are her puppies in the barn?"

He took off his hat, wiped his sleeve across his forehead and laughed. "Yeah. Dean thought he had a nice place fixed up for her at the house, but I guess she decided she liked it down here better. They're a week old now."

"Do you think she'd let me look at them?"

"Sure. Come on in." As he led her down the alleyway, Gwen inhaled the smells of hay, sweet feed, leather and the distinctive odor of manure, all reminders of happier times here with Dean.

She blinked back tears and stopped beside Emmett at the entrance to a stall. "There they are," he said. "All six of them. This is the stall where Dean keeps his horse, Midnight, but when Sadie took it over as a birthing room, he decided to let her have the whole area. Midnight had to be moved to another stall."

Sadie inched closer to Gwen, and she reached down and patted the dog's head. "Dean must really love her."

"Oh, yeah. Dean loves animals. James used to laugh and say we were going to run out of grazing space if Dean didn't quit bringing horses home. He makes it his business to find horses that have been saved from abuse and adopt them. I've lost count of how many we have now. In fact, the one you're going to ride today is a rescue horse."

"Really?"

"Dean found Princess at a shelter after she'd been taken away from a man who wouldn't feed her. She was just skin and bones when he brought her home, and she's turned out to be one of our best horses for trail rides. I've already got her saddled for you, and I'm ready to go. So let's get on the trail to Crystal Falls."

"Sounds good to me," Gwen said as she followed him toward the rear entrance of the barn. She looked back and found Sadie staring after them. The collie glanced from Gwen to her puppies before she turned and trotted into the stall.

Emmett stopped at a stall near the back and led a palomino mare out into the aisle. Gwen gasped in awe as she caught her first glimpse of Princess. Her gold coat and white mane sparkled even in the dim light of the barn.

Gwen reached out and slid her hand down the animal's mane. Princess gave a snort and nodded her head as if she approved, and Gwen felt an immediate bond with the horse.

"I'm going to enjoy riding her."

"Then let's get going," Emmett said. "Do you need any help mounting up?"

Gwen grabbed the reins, hefted her foot up to the stirrup and swung into the saddle. "I'm used to riding, so don't worry about me. I'm just eager to get started."

Thirty minutes later she closed her eyes and lifted her face up to the warm sunshine as she relaxed in the saddle. The steady rhythm of Princess's stride lulled her into an almost dreamlike state, and she couldn't remember how long it had been since she'd felt that way. It was as if the stress from the responsibilities of being a single mother and the sole breadwinner in the family had vanished, and a peace that she'd always drawn from these mountains had taken over her body.

Emmett, who was leading the way on his horse, Cocoa, swiveled in the saddle and looked back at her. "There's a small stream up ahead that we have to cross. The horses are used to the water, so don't worry."

Gwen could already hear the quiet ripple of flowing water, and she rose in the stirrups to catch a glimpse of the stream. Ahead she could see a mean-dering, shallow river dotted with rocks, and she let her gaze drift up and down the banks. She spotted several dead trees on the far side and frowned. Victims of the pollution her documentary wanted to expose?

Princess stepped into the stream, and water splashed up around Gwen's boots. Ahead of her Emmett's horse was already climbing onto the far bank. Before he could proceed any farther along the trail, Gwen called out to him, "Emmett, hold up!"

He reined in his horse and turned to look at her. "What is it?"

She nudged Princess forward and then pulled back on the reins when they reached Cocoa. Gwen swept her arm in an arc. "This is a gorgeous spot. I think it would be perfect for some location shots."

The foreman nodded. "Okay. Take all the time you need."

Gwen dismounted and pulled her cell phone from her pocket. She'd just snapped the first picture when the sudden crack of a rifle split the air. She watched in disbelief as Emmett toppled from the saddle and hit the ground.

"Emmett!" she screamed and dropped to her knees beside him.

A second shot whistled over her head, and Gwen flattened herself on the grass. With a whinny, Princess bolted back across the stream and down the trail, with Cocoa charging behind her. Gwen started to call after them, but before she could, a third shot kicked up dirt a few inches from her foot.

Emmett, blood staining the front of his shirt, pushed himself up on his knees and reached for her. "We've got to get to those trees," he said. "We need some cover."

Gwen reached down and grabbed his arm, supporting him as he staggered to his feet. Together they stumbled toward the shelter of the forest. Another bullet hit a pin oak beside them, and bark struck her face.

Gwen and Emmett scrambled toward the tree line and dived onto their stomachs into the cool darkness of the forest floor as another bullet slammed to the ground just behind them. She tugged on Emmett's arm and pulled him behind a tree, then propped her back against another one.

"How badly are you hurt?" she called out.

"I'm hit in the shoulder," he said, and a moan escaped his lips. "Call Dean and tell him what's happening. Tell him we're at Rattlesnake Creek, pinned down by a shooter."

She reached for her cell phone and then groaned in despair. The device lay at the edge of the stream, where she'd dropped it when the first shot was fired. "I lost my cell phone!"

"Mine's in my shirt pocket, but I don't think I can get it out."

Gwen debated what to do. If she left the cover of the tree where she was huddled, she might expose herself to the shooter. But if she didn't call for help, he might close in on them and kill them both. She looked at Emmett, whose shirt was becoming more blood-soaked by the minute. If she didn't do something, he might bleed to death. Her decision made, she crawled over to him and slipped his phone from his shirt pocket.

"Ranch is number one on speed dial. Somebody will answer."

"Don't worry, Emmett. Help will come." Her fingers shook so badly the phone almost slipped from her fingers.

Before it could, Emmett grabbed her hand and squeezed it. "Gun," he gasped. "G-get it out of my belt holster." He grimaced in pain and bit down on his lip. "Extra clip there, too. You know how to shoot?"

She bobbed her head in a quick nod. "Yes. Dean taught me when we were married."

The cowboy's chest rose in a quick breath. "Good. Call him. Then you gotta keep the shooter busy until help can come."

Before he could say anything else, his eyes closed and he slumped to the ground. Panicked, Gwen felt for a pulse and breathed a sigh of relief when she felt a weak one.

The front of Emmett's shirt was now soaked with his blood, and it ran down on the gun holstered on his belt. Nausea curled in Gwen's stomach. It had been several years since she'd fired a weapon. She didn't know if she could or not. As if in answer to her thought, another bullet sailed past where they lay, and she pulled the gun and the extra clip free from the holster. A quick glance told her she had fourteen shots at the most. She was going to have to space them out and make each one count until help arrived.

With shaking fingers, she aimed the gun toward

the creek and fired. A rifle shot answered, and she ducked down beside Emmett. Quickly, she punched the speed dial and held her breath, hoping someone would answer. Tears began to roll down her face when she heard Dean's familiar voice on the phone. "Emmett? I didn't expect to hear from you."

"Dean!" Gwen screamed. "We're at Rattlesnake Creek, and someone's shooting at us."

"What?" His loud voice vibrated in her ear. "Are you all right?"

"I am, but Emmett's been shot. We managed to get to some trees before he passed out, but the shooter is still out there. I have Emmett's gun. I think I can hold him off for a little while, but we need help."

The words were no sooner out of her mouth than another bullet slammed into a tree trunk near them. She screamed, and Dean shouted in her ear, "Stay where you are! I'm on my way with help!"

The call disconnected, and Gwen felt the tears washing her cheeks. Emmett's face had turned pale and his breathing was erratic. She had to do something to help slow the blood flow until Dean could arrive. She leaned over Emmett, placed her left hand on the wound and pressed down as hard as she could, hoping the pressure would help. With her right hand, she fired off another round toward their attacker.

Remember to count. That was two bullets. Don't empty both clips before Dean gets here.

As the minutes ticked by, she and the shooter played a game of call and response. He would send a shot into the forest where she and Emmett lay, and she would answer with one of her own, keeping count all the time. Then no sound or movement would occur for a few minutes. Just when she would think he must have left, another rifle crack would echo through the air, and a bullet would strike near where they lay on the forest floor. He was stringing her out deliberately, waiting for her to run out of ammunition.

How long had it been since she'd talked to Dean? Fifteen minutes? Twenty? She wasn't sure. It had taken Emmett and her thirty minutes to reach Rattlesnake Creek, but they had ridden slowly, almost at a walk. Dean would ride faster. *Don't worry. He'll be here soon*, she told herself for perhaps the tenth time.

Emmett moaned and twitched, but she released the pressure on his chest only long enough to change the clips. Suddenly she stilled and listened. The rippling gurgle that came from the river had changed. The sound of splashing water reached her ears. Someone was wading through the stream. It had to be the shooter. Her heart raced as she cowered behind the tree, Emmett's blood covering her hands.

"I'm coming for you," a singsong voice taunted from nearby.

She pressed her lips together. To respond to his jeer would reveal their hiding place, but he was headed straight for where they lay, and that meant death. Gripping the gun so tightly her knuckles turned white, she pulled the trigger twice. How many bullets did she have left now?

A shrill laugh rose from near the creek. "Too bad. Missed again. You got away yesterday, but you won't today. Won't Dean be surprised when he finds the bodies of his foreman and wife?"

How did he know she had been married to Dean? The truth suddenly dawned on her. Dean was the primary target of the killer, not her. His first victim had been Gramps, and she'd just happened on the scene. Now that this guy knew she was connected to Dean, she was also in his sights.

She raised her head enough to get a view of the stream, and her heart nearly stopped beating. A black-clothed man wearing a mask was nearing the bank, directly in line with where they lay. She aimed the gun and fired off three shots, striking the water around him. With a roar of anger, he retreated to the opposite bank, then stopped.

"I'm through playing games!" he shouted. "I'm coming to finish this off!"

Gwen released the hold on Emmett's shoulder, gripped the gun with both hands and stared down the barrel. With only two bullets left, there was no way she could fend off an attack by a killer with a rifle.

Her heart hammering, she gritted her teeth and aimed the gun toward the creek bank as she whispered a silent prayer. "Please, God. Let Dean get here before it's too late."

SEVEN

Dean's heart beat in rhythm with Midnight's thundering hooves as they raced up the trail to Rattlesnake Creek. Behind him he could hear the hoofbeats of the horses his ranch hands Luke and Jed rode. He was thankful they'd just come back from leading a trail ride when he'd swung into the saddle and yelled for them to follow him. Now they were almost there. He prayed they weren't too late to save Gwen and Emmett.

A rifle crack followed by three quick pistol shots echoed through the mountain valley, and his heartbeat quickened. He urged Midnight on faster as he squinted ahead. Just a few more yards and the creek would come into view.

He rounded the last curve in the trail. There it was, about a hundred yards away. And the sight that met his eyes impacted him like a kick to the stomach. A figure dressed in black and wearing a black ski mask stood on the bank, his gun aimed at a grove of trees on the opposite side. Before Dean could react, the man fired off a shot, and a small limb of a pine dropped to the ground.

Dean deepened his seat in the saddle, braced his legs against Midnight's sides and gave two short tugs on the reins. The horse came to an immediate stop, as he'd been trained to do. "You, there," Dean yelled as he jerked his rifle from its scabbard. "What do you think you're doing?"

The man whirled, but Dean was ready. He fired two shots in quick succession over the man's head. Startled by the sudden blast of gunfire, Midnight whinnied and shied sideways, just as a bullet whizzed past Dean's ear and struck a tree nearby. Crouching low in the saddle, he urged his mount toward the creek with Luke and Jed right behind him. The man turned and bolted into the trees behind him.

By the time they reached the stream, the shooter had disappeared into the dense growth. Dean stood up in the stirrups, waved his hand in the direction the man had gone, and yelled at Luke and Jed, "Go after him!"

The two men, almost in unison, called out the command to stop as they dropped their reins and let them dangle. With their horses ground tied, they jumped from their saddles and headed off into the woods after the shooter. Dean urged Midnight forward and splashed through the water to the opposite bank.

"Gwen! Where are you?" he called out.

"Here!" she cried, and he guided the horse toward the sound of her voice.

He stopped Midnight just short of the trees, dismounted and ducked under a low-hanging branch. As he entered the forest he saw her almost immediately. She knelt beside an unconscious Emmett, one hand pressed to his chest and the other aiming a gun at Dean.

He stopped and stretched out his arms toward her. "Honey, it's me. Dean. Put the gun down. You're safe now."

She slowly lowered the gun and dropped it to the ground, then pushed herself to her feet. "Dean..."

His gaze raked her, and his heart thudded at the sight of her clothes covered in blood. "Are you hurt?"

She closed her eyes and swayed. "No, it's Emmett's blood."

She took one step forward, but her wobbly legs wouldn't support her. As she began to sink toward the ground, Dean leaped forward and caught her. He wrapped his arms around her and pulled her shaking body close.

For a moment he held her and said a silent prayer of thanks that she'd been spared. His arms around her tightened as he breathed in the scent of the perfume she always wore. He'd thought of that smell on many lonesome nights, but he hadn't thought he would ever encounter it again.

Before he realized what he was doing, he pressed his mouth against the top of her head in a kiss. She stilled for a moment and then leaned back and stared up at him. The fear he'd seen moments ago had been replaced by something else. Regret maybe, but he couldn't be sure. Before he could say anything, she pulled free of his embrace and lowered her gaze.

Tears rolled down her cheeks. He wanted to wipe them away, but the look on her face told him that would be an unwelcome gesture. She drew a ragged breath. "I—I thought you would never get here. I d-didn't know if I could hold him off much longer. He shot Emmett, and there was so much blood."

Dean dropped to his knees next to his friend and examined the wound in his shoulder. "He's lost a lot of blood, but you did a great job taking care of both of you."

Gwen leaned against the tree where she'd been huddled with Emmett and closed her eyes. Dean wished he could pull her into his arms again and reassure her everything was going to be okay, but he wasn't sure of that. His foreman was badly wounded, and they needed to get him to a doctor as soon as possible.

"Dean!" a voice called from the direction of the creek, and she jerked erect, then whirled to stare toward the source of the sound.

"He's back!" she shrieked.

Dean jumped to his feet, and Gwen threw herself into his arms again. He hugged her close and shook his head. "No, that's Luke, one of my ranch hands. You're safe. I'm not going to let anything happen to you."

Her arms encircled his neck, and she pressed her shaking body closer. "Thank you, Dean," she whispered. "You always tried to take care of me, ever since you saved my life years ago."

Evidently her long-ago experience with the serial killer still affected her. Now, after being attacked by another murderer, she had even more bad memories to try to live with.

Glancing over her shoulder, Dean saw Luke and Jed guide their horses out of the water and onto the bank. He relaxed his hold on Gwen, who pulled away. "We're over here," he called out.

The cowboys climbed down from their horses and hurried toward them. "Sorry, boss," Luke said. "We lost his trail through the forest. This guy had to know this area well to get away from us as quick as he did."

Dean nodded. "That's what I'm afraid of. If he knows these trails, then he's been here long enough or often enough to feel at home. That's gonna make it harder to catch him. In the meantime, we've got to get Emmett to a doctor. Let's get him up on one of the horses so he can ride back to the ranch with one of you. I'll take Gwen with me."

Within minutes Luke and Jed had Emmett loaded on Luke's horse, and Luke climbed up behind. Dean swung into Midnight's saddle, reached down for Gwen and swung her up behind him. He glanced at her over his shoulder.

"Are you sure this isn't too much weight for your horse?" she asked.

He shook his head. "Midnight can handle it. Just don't hold on to me. If you started to fall off, you'd pull me with you. Then we'd both be in trouble. Hold the cantle and you'll be fine."

She nodded and gripped the back of the saddle. "I understand."

He nudged Midnight, who headed down the trail toward home. Luke and Jed followed on their horses close behind. If their mission to get Emmett to medical care hadn't been so important, Dean would have enjoyed the time with Gwen behind him on the horse he'd trained while his grandfather and Emmett had watched.

He swallowed the lump that formed in his throat at the memory of how his grandfather had leaned on the corral fence and watched as Dean worked with the young horse he'd brought home from a sale. They would never spend time like that together again. But in a few days' time, he probably wouldn't have the opportunity to be with Gwen again, either. He didn't even want to think how lonely the Little Pigeon Ranch would be when she went back to New York.

As they rode down the mountain, he looked over his shoulder from time to time to see how Luke was making it with Emmett, who had roused a bit before they started home. He appeared to be staying upright in the saddle, with Luke controlling his horse from behind. It was a good thing Dean had brought one of the best riders on the ranch along with him. Some of the others weren't experienced enough to deal with holding a wounded man in front of them on a moving horse.

Finally, the barn came in sight, and Dean breathed a sigh of relief. His truck still sat beside the corral, where he'd left it earlier. He pulled Midnight to a stop next to it and dismounted, then reached up and hauled Gwen to the ground.

A startled cry rang out, and he looked toward the barn to see Billy Champion standing just outside the door, a bucket in one hand and Princess's bridle in the other. "What happened?" he called out.

"Emmett's been shot. We have to get him to the hospital," Dean yelled back.

The bucket Billy held clattered to the ground, and he dropped Princess's reins as he ran toward them. "Who shot Emmett?"

"We don't know."

Luke and Dean dismounted and reached up to help the foreman down. Billy ran over and helped the others ease Emmett to the ground, a look of disbelief on his face as he saw the amount of blood on Emmett's shirt. "He needs to get to the hospital right away."

"Yeah," Dean said. "Let's get him in my truck." He glanced at Billy. "By the way, what are you doing here?"

"I thought you might be a little short-handed today and came over to help out. Princess came running up to the barn like she was being chased by a bear, and Cocoa came back a few minutes later. I told one of the hands we needed to go see what happened, but he said you had already left."

"Thanks for helping, Billy. It's been a wild morning around here." Dean turned to Gwen. "You go on to the house and get cleaned up. I'll call you when I know anything."

She shook her head. "No. I'm going with you. I have to make sure he's all right."

Dean's gaze raked her. "You're covered in blood, Gwen. Go change clothes." His voice sounded angrier than he'd intended.

Before he could apologize, her forehead wrinkled and she stepped closer to him. Her hands fisted at her sides, and she spoke through gritted teeth. "I imagine people at the hospital are used to seeing blood. I'm going with you." With that, she opened the extended cab door and motioned to the three men supporting Emmett. "Put him in here, and I'll climb in beside him."

They looked at Dean as if not sure what to do. "I'd forgotten how stubborn you can be," he muttered before he sighed and nodded. As the two ranch hands and Billy lifted Emmett into the vehicle, Dean hurried to the driver's side and jumped in. Gwen climbed into the back cab and crouched close to the wounded man. As soon as the door had shut, Dean turned the key in the ignition and roared down the driveway to the main road.

When he'd turned onto the highway leading into Gatlinburg, he looked over his shoulder. "Call 911 and tell them we're on our way to the hospital with a wounded man. Ask them to have Ben or a deputy meet us there."

"I dropped my cell phone in the stream."

He reached in his pocket, pulled his phone out and tossed it over the seat. "Then use mine."

Gwen caught it and punched in the number. Dean

listened as she relayed the message he'd given her. When she finished speaking, she was silent for a moment and then spoke into the phone again. "Thank you. We've just left the ranch, but we should be there shortly."

Dean glanced in the rearview mirror and could see Gwen disconnecting the call. "What did the operator say?"

"That she'd alert the hospital and have Sheriff Whitman there waiting for us."

A low moan drifted from the backseat, and Dean glanced over his shoulder quickly, then looked back at the road. "How's he doing?"

Gwen's sob answered his question. "I don't know. He's drifting in and out of consciousness. And the bleeding has increased. Please hurry, Dean."

Dean grimaced, pressed his foot on the accelerator and honked as he swerved around a car that had to be doing no more than twenty-five miles an hour. Surely the driver would realize from the flashing hazard lights and the speed he was driving that they had an emergency. Emmett had lost a lot of blood, and every minute counted right now. Dean had to get to the hospital before his friend bled to death.

He couldn't lose Emmett, too.

When Dean screeched to a stop at the emergency room entrance, Gwen was relieved to see a team of nurses waiting for them beside a gurney. She jumped out of the truck the moment it came to a halt and moved out of the way so a husky male nurse could reach inside. He lifted Emmett as if he weighed nothing and pulled him out of the backseat. With the other nurses helping, Emmett was on a gurney and being wheeled through the sliding doors at the ambulance bay before Dean had time to get out of the truck.

Dean stopped at the back and stared after them for a moment before he turned to Gwen, who was waiting for him. She started to hold out her hand, but when she glanced down, she thought better of it. Emmett's blood covered her.

"Let's go inside, Dean," she said. "I need to wash up."

He nodded, and together they walked through the entrance. She stopped just inside and looked around the waiting room. It was about half filled, with several people waiting for help. Pain flickered across the faces of some, while others sat slumped in chairs, their bored gazes fixed on the television that blared out the latest episode of a reality show.

Gwen had never liked hospitals. Not the antiseptic smell, the quiet halls with closed doors, the occasional wail of pain that could be heard or the figures in scrubs who bustled about, dispensing care to those in need. Perhaps her aversion stemmed from her memories of the night her father had died in a car crash. Even so, she needed to put that out of her mind and concentrate on matters at hand.

Her gaze dropped to her hands again, and her stomach churned. Glancing around, she spotted the sign for a restroom. "I need to get cleaned up," she repeated and headed toward it.

She pushed through the door, hurried to the sink and turned on the hot water. A container of liquid soap hung on the wall, and she lathered her hands and began to scrub. A red stream trickled from her hands as she rinsed, lathered again and scrubbed some more. She had no idea how long it took to wash away the evidence of what had happened at Rattlesnake Creek, but she finally decided she had done all she could at this point.

She pulled a paper towel from the dispenser, dried her wet skin and dropped the used towel in the trash can. Holding her hands up, she examined them for any trace of blood. When she didn't see any, she closed her eyes and felt the tears begin to trickle down her face. She might have washed the blood away, but the memory was another matter.

The terror she had experienced in the forest next to that creek wasn't something she could wash away so easily. In her mind she could still hear the bullets striking the trees and the ground around them, and the voice that had taunted her. Who was he, and why did he want to use Emmett and her to hurt Dean?

Closing her eyes, she leaned against the sink. After a few minutes she shook her head and straightened her spine. She couldn't hide in the restroom all night like a scared little girl. The sheriff should be here anytime now, and she needed to tell him what had happened.

She took a shaky breath and pulled another paper towel from the dispenser. When she'd wet it, she washed her face in an effort to soothe her red-streaked eyes and to rinse away the smudges on her cheeks, then pulled Dean's cell phone from her pocket and cleaned it. She glanced down at her jeans and shirt and swallowed the bile that flowed into her mouth at the bloodstains she saw.

There was nothing she could do about that now. She opened the door and walked back out to the waiting room. Dean leaned on the wall opposite the bathroom door, and he straightened when he spotted her.

"Here's your cell phone," she said and held it toward him.

He reached for it, then let his gaze rake her bloodstained clothes. The muscle in his jaw flexed as he slipped the device in his jeans pocket. He took a step closer. "You're all right, aren't you? You didn't get nicked by a bullet?"

His voice vibrated with concern, and her pulse quickened. For a moment all she wanted was to have him put his arm around her and kiss her hair as he had at Rattlesnake Creek. But she couldn't allow that to happen again.

"I'm not injured, Dean. I guess I'm not over my scare yet. I thought we were going to die. And we would have if you and your employees hadn't arrived."

He reached for her hand and held it between both of his. She didn't want to look down, but couldn't resist the urge. She'd been shocked yesterday when she saw that he still wore his wedding ring. She laid her free hand on top of his and rubbed the gold band that she had picked out before their wedding. Suddenly she felt as if the breath had been sucked out of her at the feeling of tremendous loss that swept through her.

She'd had the feeling many times in the past few years, but being here with Dean now made her aware of what they had once had and how it had come to a sad end. Tears stung her eyes, and she blinked.

"Gwen," he whispered, "if anything had happened to you…"

"Dean!" a voice called out, and they turned to see Ben Whitman coming toward them.

Gwen pulled her hand free and Dean sucked in a big gulp of air before he glanced at his friend. "Ben, thanks for coming. We've had some trouble out at the ranch, and I think it's related to what happened yesterday."

Ben nodded and pointed along the hallway. "There's a room down there that the hospital staff lets us use when we need to talk with someone in private. Let's go."

"Let me tell the receptionist where we will be. I want to know what the doctor says about Emmett's condition as soon as he knows anything."

Dean had no sooner finished speaking than the doors to the treatment area opened and a young man in scrubs walked toward them. He stopped beside Dean. "Mr. Harwell, I'm Dr. Owens. Your friend is doing fine. He's lost a lot of blood from the wound in his shoulder, but his vital signs are strong right now. We're on our way to surgery with him to remove the bullet. He's awake and talking, but he won't be for long. He wanted me to tell you not to worry." The doctor turned to Gwen. "And he wanted me to thank you for saving his life. In fact, he said he thought he might call you Annie from now on, after the famous Annie Oakley."

Gwen and Dean both laughed, but she sobered quickly. "He's really going to be all right, Dr. Owens?"

"He should be fine. I'll let you know as soon as he's out of surgery."

"We'll be in the conference room down the hall, Doc," Ben said.

"Good. I'll come there when I know anything."

They watched as he reentered the treatment area, and then they walked down the hallway to the conference room. When they were settled around the long mahogany table, Ben pulled a notepad and pen from his pocket and looked at Dean. "Now tell me what happened today."

"I only know the ending of the attack. Gwen was the one there from the start."

The sheriff shifted his attention to her. "All right, Miss Anderson. Suppose you tell me what happened out there."

Gwen took a calming breath. "Well, it started out as a simple trail ride. Emmett and I left the barn around ten this morning to head up to Crystal Falls. I wanted to scout out some locations for the TV documentary I'm doing."

For the next few minutes she related the events that had unfolded on their journey. When she got to the part about how she'd been running low on bullets, and the way the shooter had jeered at her from the creek, her breath hitched in her chest.

She shuddered and crossed her arms over her stomach. "His voice sounded so evil. And his words were those of a madman set on vengeance."

Ben quit writing for a moment and frowned. "Vengeance? What did he say?"

She closed her eyes, and it was as if she was back in that forest with a killer coming closer and closer. She had to force herself to answer. "He said, 'You got away yesterday, but you won't today. Won't Dean be surprised when he finds the bodies of his foreman and wife?'"

Ben's eyebrows arched. "Wife? How did he know that you were Dean's wife?"

"I don't know. I wondered the same thing. Then I realized he'd killed Dean's grandfather, and now he wants to kill his foreman and ex-wife. The only thing that makes sense is that the killer is really after…"

"Me!" Dean exclaimed. He jumped to his feet and kicked his chair backward, then strode to the far end of the room and stood for a moment, his hands propped on his hips as he stared at the wall. Finally, he turned back to Gwen.

"This is all my fault. Someone hates me and is taking it out on those I care about. First my grandfather and now you and Emmett."

Gwen pushed herself up from her chair and hurried over to Dean. She wrapped her fingers around his upper arms and gripped him tightly. "No, Dean.

This is not your fault. You can't help it if some crazy person wants to kill innocent people."

Ben stood in turn and cleared his throat. "Now hold on, you two. We don't need to go jumping to any conclusions just yet about what this killer is after. It could be that he has some reason to want to hurt you, Dean, but then, our shooter might be someone who followed Gwen here. Maybe your grandfather happened on him yesterday on that mountain trail and something happened that caused the guy to kill him."

Dean cast a skeptical glance at his friend. "That's a far-out theory, Ben."

"Well, I've done this job long enough to know that you can't rule out anything. Now think, Gwen. Is there anyone who could have followed you here?"

She shook her head. "No. There's no one."

"Yes, there is," Dean said. "Mark Dyson."

Ben jerked his attention to Dean. "Who's Mark Dyson?"

"A lawyer from Knoxville. He bumped into Gwen at her motel and has been going out of his way to be friendly since then. I discovered this morning that he's lead counsel for a company that Gwen's documentary is about to expose for endangering the environment."

"Mark Dyson," Ben murmured as he wrote the name down. "Where can we find him?"

Gwen started to protest, but something told her not to. They needed to let Ben follow every lead if they were to catch this killer. "He's staying at the Mountain View Motel."

Ben pulled his phone from his pocket, turned his back to them and punched in a number. "Martha," he said. "This is Ben. Tell Deputy Bridges to go to the Mountain View Motel and check out a guy named Mark Dyson. I want to know where he was all day and what he was doing. I want Bridges on this now, top priority, and he's to call me as soon as he knows anything."

Ben disconnected the call and turned back to them. "He'll check this out right away."

"So what shall we do while we wait?" Gwen asked.

The sheriff turned to Dean. "I need to know the rest of the story. What happened after you arrived at the creek?"

Dean nodded and began to relate how hard he and his ranch hands had ridden to get to Gwen and Emmett, how he'd exchanged fire with the shooter before he disappeared into the forest, and how they'd got Emmett back to the barn as quickly as possible.

"Then we loaded him up and brought him here," Dean stated.

As Gwen listened, she could hear Dean's respect and affection for Emmett in his words, and she knew he was deeply worried about his friend. She studied his handsome profile as he spoke and began to realize that he was not only the best-looking man she'd ever known, but he was also once again the good, kind man she had married.

Somewhere during their time together they had lost each other. She'd become obsessed with succeeding in her job, and he'd turned to alcohol to drown the torment his own job had caused. Maybe there was something she could have done to help him. Had she been so focused on her own needs that she had let those of her husband go unnoticed?

As she sat here listening to him, she realized he was happy now. He was free of the addiction that had once ruled his life and seemed fully determined that it would never consume him again. That thought made her happier than anything had in years, and she found herself wishing there was some way that she, Dean and Maggie could be a family. But she didn't think that would ever be possible. Just telling him about Maggie would be enough to alienate him forever.

Her thoughts were interrupted by the ringing of Ben's cell phone. "Hello?" he said.

She and Dean both scooted to the edge of their chairs and waited as he nodded and listened to what the caller was saying. After a few minutes he exhaled. "Okay. Thanks for checking this out. I'll see you at the station later."

"What did he say?" Dean asked the minute Ben completed the call.

"Bridges said that he talked with Mark Dyson. The man teed off at the Hurricane Mills Golf Club at ten o'clock this morning and was there until midafternoon. He provided the names of three men he was with. My deputy has talked to all three, and they have corroborated his alibi. So it looks like he's not our shooter."

Dean's shoulders hunched, and he rubbed the back

of his neck. "So that means I'm definitely the one the killer's after, not Gwen."

Ben shook his head. "We don't know for sure yet, pal. Give us time to work on this."

Dean stared into space for a moment before he turned to Gwen and sighed. "Okay, but in the meantime, there's only one thing to do now."

"What?" she asked.

"You have to leave. Go back home. The next time this guy may not miss."

Her mouth dropped open, and she wrapped her hands around his upper arms. "Go home? No. I'm not going to leave you alone at a time like this."

Dean shook her hands free and gritted his teeth. "You left me alone five years ago, and you've been quick to point out that nothing has changed since then. I don't need you here to pretend to care what happens to me. So I want you on the first plane out of Knoxville bound for New York tomorrow."

His words felt like a stinging slap, and tears pooled in her eyes as she recoiled from the anger in his. She couldn't believe the things he was saying. "Dean, please. I don't want to leave yet."

"That doesn't matter. When we get back to the ranch, I want you to pack your bags and be ready to go in the morning. This isn't your home, Gwen. You need to get back to New York and get on with your life there."

With that, Dean stormed through the door and into the hallway. She fought the urge to run after him, to make him explain why he was so angry with her. Ever since she'd arrived at the ranch, Dean had thrown subtle hints that he wished they could get back together. Her uncertainty over whether she could trust him again, mingled with her guilt over how she'd deceived him, had kept her from returning his interest. Maybe she'd played her part too well, and now he was through with her.

Whatever had changed his mind, she wasn't welcome at Little Pigeon Ranch anymore. If that was the case, she'd be on that plane tomorrow and would never come back to the only place that had ever seemed like home to her.

EIGHT

An hour later Dean hadn't returned, and there had been no word from the doctor. Gwen stopped pacing back and forth in the conference room and shook her head. "Why haven't we heard anything? Do you think something could have gone wrong?"

Ben frowned. "Waiting's hard, I know. I do it all the time with families of crime victims. The doctor said he'll let us know, and he will. In the meantime, how about some coffee? I'll be glad to go to the dining room and get us some."

Gwen looked down at her watch and frowned. She hadn't realized it had got so late. As if to remind her that she hadn't eaten lunch, her stomach growled. "Coffee sounds great," she said. "Could you get a snack of some kind to go with it? I don't have any money with me, but I'll repay you later."

He gave a lopsided grin and waved his hand in dismissal. "No need to do that. I'll be glad to get you something. Be back in a few minutes."

"Thanks, Sheriff Whitman."

He grinned again. "Ben."

Gwen studied the chiseled features of the man she'd met yesterday, and the tension she'd felt in her body ever since that first shot was fired at Rattlesnake Creek seemed to disappear at the kindness of his smile. Her rigid muscles relaxed, and she took a slow step toward him. "Do you really wait with all the crime victims' families who are brought here, or just special ones?"

His face turned red, and he shrugged. "Maybe not all of them, but you're different."

She frowned. "Why am I different?"

"I met Dean the first day he came to school here, right after his grandparents brought him home with them. He's been my friend ever since. I was away in the army when you two got married, and I never was home when you visited. But we kept up with each other. When he came back here five years ago, he wasn't the man I remembered."

Gwen shook her head. "No, I don't suppose he was."

"His grandfather had been telling me for several years how worried he was about Dean, said he was drinking too much. When I saw him after he came back, he was still fighting his alcoholism, but he *was* fighting—he wasn't letting it take over anymore. And that was the main thing. My church had a group to help alcoholics, and I talked him into going with me."

Her eyebrows arched. "With you? Why were you going?"

He smiled that slow smile that seemed to put her

at ease. "Because I was a recovering alcoholic, too. Became one while I was in the army, but I had gotten help and was moving on with my life. I wanted Dean to get it, too. So he finally went with me, and I became his sponsor. I was there with him when he went through his worst times, and we formed a bond like nothing I've ever had with another person. We both know what it's like to hit rock bottom and make the long, slow climb back to a happy life."

Tears pooled in Gwen's eyes, and she reached out and grasped his hand. "Thank you for being there for him, Ben. I'm so glad he had someone to hang on to during that time."

Dean's friend tilted his head to one side. "It wasn't just me, you know, who helped him through it."

"Oh? Who else helped him?"

"You."

The single word shocked her, and she frowned. "I don't understand. We were divorced, and I was nowhere around. How did I help him?"

"You were the reason he kept fighting his addiction. He set his mind on overcoming what he'd thought was impossible, because he wanted something much more important in his life. He wanted you. Every time he'd start to slip, he'd look down at his wedding ring, which he'd never taken off, and would find the strength to resist the urge to take a drink. I think you probably did more to help him than I did."

A tear slipped from the corner of her eye and ran down her cheek. "I can't imagine what that time must have been like for him and for you. Dean didn't drink when we were first married. He was the most wonderful man I'd ever known, but his job destroyed him. All I could do was love him and try to make the hours he was home good for him."

Ben exhaled a deep sigh. "Yeah, he's told me how hard it was working undercover, infiltrating the drug scene in Oxford."

"He would be gone for days," Gwen murmured. "Then he'd come home, and he'd be so stressed out that all he wanted to do was drink and forget about what he'd seen and done. I tried to get him to share his feelings with me, but he refused. He said he didn't want to upset me by telling me about the things he had to do on a daily basis. Then when the Trip King case exploded, Dean went off the deep end. He stayed drunk all the time he was at home, and he started having horrible nightmares. When I woke up one night with his hands around my throat, I thought he was going to choke me to death before I could get away. Thankfully, I was able to wake him up before he did."

Ben was silent for a moment before he nodded. "Yeah, he told me about that. It's something he can't put out of his mind. But he's never told me all the details of what sent him over the edge. You said it was the Trip King case. What happened with that?"

Gwen closed her eyes for a moment and sank down in a chair. "That was a terrible time." She crossed her arms on the conference table and tried to fight the powerless feeling that engulfed her every time she recalled the case that Dean never could forget.

Ben leaned forward. "What happened?"

She thought for a moment about where she should start, and then she swallowed. "People who live in other parts of the country don't realize how popular rodeo is in the South. There are colleges with student teams that compete in the National Intercollegiate Rodeo Association and there's a High School Rodeo Association for younger riders. Small towns all over the area sponsor yearly events for professional competitors. One of the most followed sports is bull riding."

Ben grinned. "Yeah. I competed as a bronc rider when I was younger."

"Then you know how seriously the sport is taken. Trip King was a young man who'd been a star bull rider on his college team. He was the son of a single mother, and he went to school on scholarships. Not only was he a gifted rider with movie-star good looks, but he was smart. Graduated with high honors, and he was on his way to a successful life." Gwen paused for a moment.

"Go on," Ben said.

"After he graduated, he went on the pro rodeo circuit and began to gain attention from promoters. Soon he had lined up some endorsements, and he was gaining points in competitions that were inching him up the ladder to take over the number one spot in the championship bull-riding standings. Then he came to Oxford for the annual rodeo there, and that's where it happened."

"What?"

"Dean wasn't supposed to be working that night, but he took the shift of a fellow officer who needed to be at the hospital with his sick child. The police got a tip that there were a lot of drugs being sold around the stadium where the rodeo was being held, so Dean and another officer went to check it out. They soon discovered that Trip King was the head drug dealer. When they approached him, he panicked and tried to run. They followed, and he pulled a gun from his truck and shot the officer with Dean—a man Dean had known for years. He died instantly."

She stopped talking for a moment and thought of that officer and the wife and two children he'd left behind. Her heart ached once again, just as it had then. "Dean did what he was trained to do. He returned fire, and Trip King was killed." She glanced up at Ben and shook her head. "After that there was nothing I could do to help him. He was so burdened with guilt that he refused to see that he'd had no choice. Even after the official investigation into the case showed that Dean acted in accordance with police standards and he wasn't held responsible for the shooting, he couldn't accept it. He kept saying that Trip King was just a kid who'd been influenced by the wrong people. He was on his way to becoming a big-time star with a huge earning potential, and he even had movie agents trying to sign him. The future was his, and Dean felt like he'd taken it away from him."

Ben pursed his lips and stared off into space for a few moments before speaking. "It's a hard thing to take someone's life, even in the line of duty. I can understand what Dean must have gone through. I know that he hasn't forgotten that case, although he won't talk to me about it."

"The night Dean pulled the trigger and shot Trip King, he killed our marriage, too. From that time on he spiraled further and further down into alcoholism. After he almost killed me, I knew it was time to leave. I did the only thing I could. I divorced him."

"And made him promise to never look for you."

Gwen swallowed the lump in her throat. "Yes."

"And he never did." Ben paused and directed a somber look at her. "He always told me that if God wanted the two of you back together, He'd work it out."

Gwen rose to her feet, shook her head and walked to the other end of the room. Without turning around, she clenched her fists at her sides as she stared at the wall in front of her. "God had nothing to do with my being here," she rasped. "It was just a coincidence that I saw his grandfather's body being dumped in that stream. Now Dean says I have to leave, and I think he's right. I plan to be gone first thing tomorrow. I hope you find whoever killed his grandfather and tried to kill Emmett and me. But I won't be here to see it happen. I'm going home, where I belong, and I don't want to ever hear from Dean again."

She whirled around, then gasped. Dean had quietly reentered the room and stood next to Ben. A sad expression lined his face as he let his gaze travel over her. All of a sudden she felt as if she would suffocate from the heavy tension that hung in the conference room. She couldn't speak, but only stare at him.

After a moment he pulled his eyes away and turned to Ben. "I met the doctor in the hall. Emmett came through his surgery fine and is in recovery. They're going to move him into the critical care unit for overnight observation, and we can see him for a few minutes in another hour or so."

The sheriff glanced at his watch. "Then I don't think I'll wait. I have some work to do at the office before the next shift change. I have Gwen's statement about what happened and yours concerning what you saw after you arrived at the creek. I'll come back in the morning to talk to Emmett. Maybe he'll be feeling more up to remembering details then."

"That's okay," Dean said. "No need for you to hang around here. So if you're leaving, would you mind taking Gwen back to the ranch? She needs to get packed so she can go home in the morning."

"Sure," Ben said. "I'll be glad to."

Gwen frowned and shook her head. "Dean, I'll stay. I want—"

He held up a hand to stop her. "Please just go, Gwen. I'll be home later, and I'll try to see you before you leave tomorrow."

Her heart pounded in her chest. She couldn't believe what he was saying. He was sending her on her way as if she was some unwanted ranch guest he couldn't wait to be rid of. She lifted her chin and glared at him. "You'll *try* to see me in the morning? Very well. If that's the way you want it."

He nodded. "That's the way I want it."

She straightened her spine and walked toward the door. "Then let's go, Ben. I have some packing to do."

She didn't look back as she walked from the conference room and out the emergency room doors toward the squad car. Neither she nor Ben spoke as he pulled out of the parking lot and drove toward the ranch.

After a few miles, he exhaled and glanced her way. "Gwen, I'm sorry. Dean wasn't trying to hurt you. He's trying to protect you. He wants you gone so the killer won't target you again. I'm sure you'll hear from him after we catch this guy."

"I don't *want* to hear from him again. I've told him ever since I got here that I don't want to recapture what we once had. The past is dead and gone. I have another life now, and I can't ever have one with Dean."

"*Can't?* That's a strange word to use. Do you not want to have a life with Dean, or is there some reason that you *can't* have one with him?"

"It doesn't matter," she murmured. "There's no going back."

She turned her head and stared out the window as they traveled over the winding mountain road to Little Pigeon Ranch. She tried to memorize every inch of the rolling landscape so she would have something on sleepless nights to remind her of how happy she'd once been.

Finally, she leaned her forehead against the window and closed her eyes. *Please, God, help me. I know I was wrong not to tell Dean about Maggie.*

But what do I do now? He deserves to know he has a daughter and to have a relationship with her. But he will hate me for keeping her a secret. Tell me what to do.

The car hit a bump in the road, and her head bounced back and then struck the window again. It was as if the jolt had produced the answer she'd prayed for. The only way she was ever going to gain any peace from the guilt she carried was to face up to the mistake she'd made five years ago.

Before she left, she had to tell Dean he had a daughter, and Gwen had to ask his forgiveness for keeping her from him. Then all she could do was depend on God to give her strength to face the repercussions that would surely follow her confession.

Dean sat in a chair in the corner of the critical care waiting area and sipped at a cup of coffee that had grown cold since he'd bought it an hour ago. It was after ten o'clock, and so far he'd been allowed one short visit with Emmett. That was enough to assure him that the man who'd been his grandfather's right hand for years was going to recover from his wound.

The doctor and nurses had told him to go home, that there was nothing else he could do tonight. For some reason, though, he couldn't bring himself to leave. Emmett had no family, and Dean couldn't stand the thought of him being alone and hurt without someone who cared close by. Maybe if Emmett was better in the morning, Dean could go home and get some sleep.

He glanced around the room and saw that most of the

people keeping vigil tonight for their loved ones were beginning to settle down on the chairs and couches scattered throughout the area. Nurses' aides had distributed pillows and blankets to everyone about thirty minutes ago, and already some soft snores drifted across the room.

He heard movement at the door and glanced up to see Ben walking into the room, a paper bag from a local fast-food restaurant in his hand. He came over to where Dean sat and dropped down in the chair next to him.

"I figured you probably hadn't eaten anything. So I stopped at your favorite hamburger place and got you something."

Dean inhaled the burger's smell and smiled as his stomach growled. "I was getting a little hungry." He pulled out the sandwich, unwrapped the foil and took a big bite. "Mmm, that's good," he said after he'd chewed and swallowed. "I didn't realize I was starving."

Ben chuckled and settled back in his chair. "How's Emmett doing?"

"The doctor says he'll be fine. They tried to get me to go on home, but I didn't want to leave him."

"I'm sure they'll call you if there's any change. Go on home and get some rest."

Dean shook his head, took another bite and washed it down with a swig of coffee. "Can't do it. I have to make sure he's okay before I leave."

"There's somebody else you need to make sure is okay, too."

Dean put the rest of the burger back in the sack and heaved a deep sigh. "Are you talking about Gwen?"

"Yeah. I saw how happy you were when she showed up here. Now you're in a hurry to make her leave. She's confused."

"But you understand why I want her gone, don't you?"

His friend nodded. "Of course I do. You want to protect her from this killer who's targeted her. Sending her home is a way of doing that."

"Then what's the problem?"

Ben sighed and swiveled in his seat to face Dean. "The problem, buddy, is that *she* doesn't understand. You need to explain it to her. Send her back to New York, but tell her you'd like to see her again when this is all over, that you want to work things out between the two of you."

Dean shook his head. "That wouldn't do any good. She's got this guy back East. It sounds like he's well-off. Has a house with horses out in the Hamptons. He'll be able to give her a better life than I ever could."

"Not if the two of you love each other."

"That's just it, Ben. She doesn't love me anymore, and I don't have anybody but myself to blame. I ruined it for us years ago, and I guess I need to accept the truth once and for all. There's no going back."

Ben didn't say anything as he stretched out his long legs, crossed them at the ankles and slumped in his chair. Then he shrugged. "Well, I guess I can't make you do what you don't want to. But what I know is that you can't bring yourself to take off your wedding ring, even though you were divorced five years ago. And I remember that the only reason you got through all those nights that I sat with you when you were trying to beat your addiction was because you wanted Gwen to know that you could be a different man. Somebody she could love again."

"I know that, but—"

"And I also know," Ben continued as if he hadn't heard him, "that you said God would work it out if the two of you were meant to be together." He heaved himself up out of his chair and grasped Dean's shoulder. "God saw you through those rough times, and now He's given you the chance to try for happiness again. Don't throw that away because you're afraid. I don't know what she'll say, and neither do you. You'll never know if you're too scared to find out. Don't let this opportunity slip through your fingers. It may not come again. I'll check on Emmett in the morning."

The lawman patted him on the shoulder once more and walked from the room. Dean stared after him until he'd moved out of sight, then bent forward and covered his face with his hands. Everything Ben had said was true. Dean had loved Gwen from the first time he saw her, and that hadn't changed. Ben was also right that getting her back had been the driving force helping Dean recover sobriety. The thought that she might love him again someday had got him through some of the worst times that a human should have to endure.

During those times he'd poured out his heart to God and begged for the right to have another chance with her. Now she was staying at his ranch, and he was afraid to say the things he'd been planning for years. On the other hand, he'd told her that he knew God had brought her here, and she had dismissed the idea. Maybe he should, too, and just let her go back and pick up her life with someone else.

Dean stood and walked out into the hall. The only sounds were soft voices that drifted from the vending room to his left, and he stopped and glanced in. A man and a woman sat on a couch. They held each other's hands as if they needed a lifeline, and from the words they were speaking, Dean knew they did. At that moment they were reaching out to the only source that could help them.

"God, please don't take him away from us," he heard the man say above the soft sobs of the woman. "He's our only child. Please let him live."

Dean closed his eyes for a moment and remembered the nights he'd struggled and begged God to deliver him from his addiction. God had done that. If that could happen, He could heal Dean's marriage, too. But he had to step out in faith and see where it led him.

The man on the couch ended his prayer and pulled his wife close, then glanced up. Dean bit down on his lip at the sorrow he saw in the man's eyes. "What's your son's name?" Dean asked.

The woman twisted in her husband's arms and smiled through her tears. "His name is Jason. He's sixteen years old, and he had an accident on a four-wheeler this afternoon. The doctors aren't sure if he'll make it or not."

Dean walked into the room, squatted down in front of them and laid a hand on the shoulder of each. "Let me pray with you, too."

The man inhaled a quick breath and wiped at his eyes. "We'd like that."

Dean closed his eyes and wrinkled his forehead as he began to pray. "Dear God, waiting is hard, and these fine folks are suffering right now. I pray that You will give them strength to face their fears and comfort them with the knowledge that they're not alone. I know that You can heal Jason and restore him to his parents, and I pray that You will do that. The Bible tells us to ask and it shall be given, so in the quiet of this room I ask that You heal Jason. And we will give You the praise forever. Amen."

As he finished the prayer, the woman began to sob louder, and she grabbed him in a fierce hug. "Thank you…"

"Harwell. Dean Harwell. I hope you have good news soon."

All three of them rose to their feet, and the man grabbed Dean's hand. "We're Steve and Betty Price. Thank you, Mr. Harwell, for praying for our son."

"I'll keep praying for him, too. I have to go now, but I'll be back in the morning to check on my friend who's in the unit. I'll check on Jason then. Now you need to try and get some sleep tonight. When Jason gets better, he's going to need you to be at your healthiest so you can take care of him."

Betty smiled. "Thank you for saying *when*, not *if.*"

"Keep praying," Dean said.

With that, he walked from the room and headed toward the exit. He stopped outside the door and stared up at the stars as he thought about the Prices. They'd had no idea when they got up this morning that they would be praying for their son's life before the day was over, but they were. They reinforced the truth that no one knew what the future might hold, and it was no use worrying about what might happen.

Dean had wasted enough time. He needed to let Gwen know how much he loved her and that he wanted her back. She might reject him, but at least he would have tried.

When he got to his truck, he climbed in and was just about to start the engine when he heard the chime of a text coming in on his phone. He pulled it from his pocket and frowned at the unknown number displayed.

The words of the text almost jumped off the screen at him. It's too early to celebrate the Fourth of July, but I thought you might enjoy some fireworks at your place tonight.

For a moment he couldn't move as he read the message. Fireworks at his ranch tonight? That sounded like a threat—no doubt from the shooter. A chill went down Dean's spine, and the hair on the back of his neck stood up. Gwen! He'd sent her back to the ranch! He had to warn her.

He had punched in the first three digits of her cell number when he remembered she'd lost hers at Rattlesnake Creek. With a groan, he ended the call and tried the ranch phone instead. At this time of night Shorty and the rest of the ranch hands would probably be asleep in the bunkhouse.

When the call went to voice mail, he hit speed dial for Ben's number. His friend answered right away. "Hey, Dean, what's up?"

"I just got a text from someone saying that there were going to be fireworks at my ranch tonight. Do you have a deputy in the area who can meet me there?"

"Yeah, Hughes is out that way. I'll meet you, too."

"Thanks," Dean said. He tossed the cell phone in the center console cup holder and turned on the ignition. The tires screeched as he roared out of the parking lot and onto the road that led out of town.

"Please, God," he prayed as he drove. "Let her be all right. Give me the chance to tell her I love her."

NINE

Gwen checked her suitcase one last time to make sure she had everything packed. She hadn't been at the ranch long enough to have scattered her belongings, but she wanted to make sure she was in her rental car in the morning and ready to be on her way to Knoxville as soon as she finished the conversation with Dean she couldn't put off any longer.

Looking back on the decision she'd made not to tell him about his daughter, she now wished she had handled the situation differently. Maybe knowing that he had someone to love would have made his recovery easier. At the time, however, all she had thought about was protecting herself and her child from the man he'd become.

Now that Gwen had seen how his life had turned out, she knew she had to tell him about Maggie. He would hate her when he found out, but that was the punishment she'd have to endure for the choice she'd made. At least he could have someone to love, and Maggie could have all her questions about the father she'd never known answered.

Gwen glanced around the room again to see if she'd forgotten to pack anything and to make sure she'd laid out the clothes she intended to wear tomorrow. There wouldn't be time to do any last-minute packing. When she confessed to Dean, she needed to be ready to leave. It might be a good idea to have her suitcases in the car even before she talked to him.

She started to pick up the bags to take them out there when a loud, piercing sound seemed to shake the house. She dropped the suitcases and ran to the door. A couple staying two rooms down from her opened their door and hurried into the hall.

The woman clutched the front of her robe closed. Her husband stared at Gwen with wide eyes. "What's that sound?" he asked.

"I don't know, but I'll find out."

She ran to the staircase and grabbed the banister as she rushed down the stairs. The sound grew more intense the lower she went. When she reached the ground floor, she realized the blaring siren was coming from the direction of the office.

Suddenly she knew she was hearing the fire alarm from the barn being broadcast over the intercom, and her stomach churned. Princess, Midnight and Cocoa, as well as half a dozen other horses, would be in their stalls. There was no time to waste.

She grabbed the desk phone and punched in 911. An operator answered immediately.

"This is 911. What is your emergency?"

"There's a fire at Little Pigeon Ranch," she screamed into the phone. "We need help."

"That fire's already been reported, ma'am, and the trucks are on the way. They should be there any minute now."

"Thanks!" Gwen cried and slammed the phone back in its cradle.

Then she turned and ran out of the house and toward the barn. She could see a faint glow coming from inside it, and her breath hitched in her throat as she got closer. She stopped at the entrance as Shorty hurried out, leading one of the horses she'd seen earlier today.

"Can I help?" she yelled.

He handed her the rope he held. "Take this horse and put him in the corral. We need to get the horses as far away from the fire as possible. Be careful he doesn't get spooked. Horses have a tendency to run back to the safety of their stalls. We don't need to be chasing 'em down after we've got them out."

Gwen took the rope. "Do you need me to help get the rest of the horses out of the barn?"

He shook his head. "It's best you let us handle that," he called out as he headed back. "Several of the men are in there now getting the horses. We always keep each horse's bridle with a cotton lead hanging outside the stall for emergencies like this. Don't worry. We'll get all of them."

For the next few minutes Gwen hurried back and forth between the barn and corral, leading rescued horses to safety. She was on her way back after releasing another horse when one of the ranch hands rushed past her leading a mare.

"This is the last one. They're all out."

Gwen gave a sigh of relief and trudged back to the front of the barn. The flames appeared to be brighter now. In the distance she could hear the sirens of approaching fire trucks. Maybe they'd be able to save some of the structure.

She stopped a good distance away from the entrance and stared at the flames. She sensed movement next to her and turned her head to see Billy Champion standing beside her. "Billy, what are you doing here?"

"The wind must have been just right to carry the sound of the fire alarm to my place. When I heard it, I knew exactly what it was, and I came as quickly as I could to help. Shorty tells me all the horses are safe."

Gwen nodded. "Yes, they are, and all the ranch hands got out safely." She tilted her head and studied the flames again. "The fire is burning slower than I thought it would have. I would expect a wooden barn to burn much quicker."

"Most would," Billy said. "But Dean's a smart man. He had some remodeling done a few years ago and had the entire place covered with a flame-retardant paint. Then he had a solid floor-to-ceiling partition built after every fourth stall. That's kept the flames from jumping from one section to another. Just a few things like that can make the difference between a barn lasting long enough for the firefighters to get there or burning to the ground in a few minutes."

"It's a good thing that he…" Gwen stopped when she heard a sound near her feet. She glanced down to find Sadie beside her, staring at the barn and whining. The collie looked up at her and barked, then ran toward the barn, turned and barked again.

"What is it, girl?" Gwen asked, kneeling when the dog came back and putting her arm around her.

At that moment a truck roared off the road and came to a screeching stop beside the house. The door opened, and Dean jumped out. He ran toward the barn, where he was met by Shorty and several other men. Gwen was near enough to hear their conversation.

"Are all the horses safe?" Dean asked.

"We got them all out, boss," one of the cowboys said. "They're all in the corral."

Dean looked over his shoulder as the first fire truck rolled into the yard. "Good. Then let's get out of the way and let the firemen do their job." He turned and spotted Gwen, and his gaze dropped to the collie beside her. "What about Sadie's puppies?" he asked Shorty.

The men all looked at him with blank faces. "We didn't think about them," Shorty said.

Gwen gasped and gazed into the dark eyes of the shaking dog she still held. "Sadie's puppies!" she exclaimed. She jumped to her feet and grabbed Billy by the arm. "That's what's wrong with Sadie. Her puppies are still in there."

He looked back at the firemen, who were just beginning to unroll their water hoses. "Don't worry. They'll get them."

Just then a loud popping sound split the air, and a new burst of heat gushed from inside the barn. "The fire's spreading!" Gwen cried. "We've got to get the puppies before it's too late."

She took a step, but Billy grabbed her arm and pulled her back. "You can't go in there."

"I have to! I can't let those puppies die!"

She shook free of his hand and raced toward the barn, her heart pounding. Behind her she heard Billy shouting, "Dean! Gwen has gone in the barn to get the puppies!"

She ignored his cries and rushed headlong into the burning building. The heat that enveloped her sucked the breath from her body, but she staggered on toward Midnight's stall at the back, where she'd seen the puppies earlier today.

Smoke boiled around her, burning her eyes, but she didn't stop. She heard the whimpers of the puppies before she reached the stall and stumbled inside. Tears rolled down her face from the stinging in her eyes, and she dropped on her knees beside the wriggling animals. Only then did she realize her mistake. How could she carry six puppies out of here? There was certainly no time to make two trips.

She grabbed two of the dogs and was trying to decide how to carry the other four when she heard someone running down the alleyway. Dean burst through the stall door, grabbed her by the arm and jerked her to her feet. "Are you crazy, coming into a burning barn?"

She swallowed and ignored the anger she could see in his eyes. "Save it for later, Dean. Grab some of those puppies, and let's get out of here."

He reached down and picked up two of the dogs

as Billy Champion charged through the stall door. "Give me two! We need to go!"

With all six puppies in their arms, they ran toward the door, past flames that were growing more intense by the moment, and outside into the cool night air. As they exited, Sadie ran toward them, barking at the top of her lungs, and began to jump up in an effort to reach her babies. The firemen aimed the first stream of water at the barn, and the three of them stopped a safe distance away and set the puppies down.

Sadie whined and licked each one as if to reassure herself that they were okay, and Gwen smiled at the sight, until she looked up at Dean. His eyes flashed with anger, and she sucked in her breath. She'd never seen him as livid as he appeared to be at this minute.

Shorty rushed up and started to speak, but after looking at Dean, he seemed to think better of it. "Let's get these puppies to a safe place, Billy," he said as he reached down and picked up three of them.

Billy nodded and grabbed the other three, then walked quickly away with the cook, Sadie following. When the men were out of earshot, Dean turned his attention back to Gwen. "Do you realize you could have been killed?"

"Dean, please listen—" she began, but he was having none of it.

He held up his hand to stop her. "You've been back in my life for two days now, and it's been nothing but one crisis after another."

Her own anger flared, and she clenched her fists at her sides. "That hasn't been my fault," she snarled.

"Then whose fault is it that you disregarded your safety, as well as mine and Billy's, to run into a burning barn?"

She took a step closer and glared at him. "I didn't ask you to come after me. That was your choice."

"And I wouldn't have had to make it if you'd used some common sense and let the firemen take care of the puppies."

"Oh, so that's it, is it? You're angry not because I was in danger but because you might have been hurt."

His eyes widened as if she had slapped him. "That's not true!" he cried.

They were almost nose to nose now. "Then what is the truth?" she yelled into his face.

He leaned even closer and shouted, "The truth is that I love you, and it's tearing me apart having you here. When I saw you go in that barn, I thought I'd die if anything happened to you." He stumbled a few steps back and stared at her, no longer angry, now looking defeated.

"You love me?" she whispered.

He rubbed his hands over his face and groaned. "I always have, from that first moment I saw you, and that won't ever change. I'm sorry that I shouted at you just now, but I was so scared you were about to be killed. And I'm sorry about what I said at the hospital. I don't want you to leave. I want you to stay. Forever." He reached out and put his hands on either side of her face as he stared down into her eyes. "You're the only person I love who I have left in my life. Please don't leave me again. Stay and let's try to find our way back to each other."

Before she could answer, Shorty ran up. "Dean, Ben just got here. He and the fire chief want to talk with you. They think the barn fire was arson."

He sighed and nodded. "I'm sure it was. I received a text that it was about to happen."

"You what?" Gwen exclaimed.

He turned back to her and touched her arm. "Go on back to the house, Gwen. I'll meet you in the office in a few minutes. We need to finish this conversation."

She nodded. "Yes, we do."

Dean and Shorty turned and walked back toward the barn, and she watched them go. He was right. It was time for them to have a serious conversation, but she didn't think he was going to like what she had to say.

A tear rolled out of her eye, and she wiped it away. She'd known from the minute she'd opened her eyes in that ambulance that she'd never stopped loving Dean, and now he said he still loved her, too. But that was about to change, and she had nobody to blame but herself.

Dean watched Gwen trudge back toward the house and frowned. She didn't seem very happy that he'd just laid his heart out to her and told her he loved her. He had hoped she might want to try again. Now he wasn't so sure. Her reaction to his admission that he loved her hadn't produced any hint that she might feel the same. He supposed he might as well get ready to be rejected when they talked.

Right now, though, there was the question of the barn. They had to find out who was targeting him, and soon. With his grandfather's murder, three attempts on Gwen's life and now a burning barn, there was no telling what the killer had in mind next.

Ben and the fire chief, Keith Davidson, stood apart from the rest of the first responders and appeared to be involved in a serious discussion as he approached. Ben glanced up when Dean stopped beside him.

"I'm sorry about your barn, Dean. I understand they got all the animals out, though."

"Yeah." He grunted and rubbed the back of his neck. "I'm thankful for that and that none of my staff were injured trying to rescue them. Whoever's after me isn't giving up."

Ben nodded. "Seems that way. Let me see the text you told me you received."

Dean pulled his cell phone from his pocket and handed it over. When the sheriff finished reading the text, he handed it to the fire chief. "I'd call that a threat. What do you think, Keith?"

The chief read it and then nodded. "Well, you've certainly had fireworks here tonight, and they didn't happen accidentally."

"Are you sure it's arson?" Dean asked.

"I'm about 95 percent certain at this point, but we'll know after we start our investigation."

Dean studied his burning barn for a few moments before he spoke again. "I used to know some guys who were firefighters. They were always talking about the different methods they had of determining if a fire was started on purpose. I know the text I got points to it being arson, but do you have any other evidence?"

"Just observation," Keith said. "From what we saw when we arrived, it looked like the flames were the same at multiple locations in the barn. That could mean it was set in different places. Also, the fires appeared to be burning down instead of up. If an accelerant was used around the stalls, it would have soaked into the wood and would have burned down toward the ground. We'll know more about where it all started when we can follow the char pattern."

Dean nodded. "You think you'll be able to find it under all the ash that'll be left?"

"Oh, yeah. We often find clues when we clear away the ash. A fire leaves definite footprints. We'll follow them until we have the origins and the cause."

Dean rubbed his hands over his eyes and sighed. "Just let me know what you find out. I'll get in touch with my insurance company in the morning. I'm sure their investigators will want to be in on this, too."

"Tell them to get in touch with me," Keith said. "Now I need to check on my guys. I'll talk to you later."

As the chief walked away, Ben turned to Dean. "Are you okay, buddy? I know this has been a horrible blow."

Dean sighed. "Yeah, especially since this is peak tourist season." He glanced at the guests who'd gathered to watch the fire. "I'm not sure we even have enough equipment left to outfit a trail ride. I guess I'll be sending all the guests home in the morning and contacting the ones with reservations to tell them what happened. Insurance should cover the barn and equipment, but there are my employees to think about. They have to be paid even though I won't have any money coming in. On top of that, I've never had to shoulder the full load of running the ranch completely on my own before."

His throat closed and he swallowed. "I sure do wish Granddad was here. Even when he was too sick to help with the day-to-day tasks, he was always around to encourage me and give me advice."

Ben stuck his hands in his pockets and squinted as he stared at the flames again. "We're all going to miss James. But I'm going to do everything I can to catch his killer and whoever set this fire."

"I know you will. What about Mark Dyson? Even though the lead on the shooting didn't pan out, maybe you need to see if he has an alibi tonight."

"I've already thought of that. Hughes went by the motel and learned that he'd checked out this afternoon. He called the home phone number Dyson had given when questioned earlier, and the man answered. He said he'd been home for the last three hours, and his wife backed him up. He couldn't have set this fire if he was in Knoxville at the time."

"I guess not," Dean said. "Do you think you might be able to find out where the text came from by checking the cell-phone records?"

"I'll take care of that right away. Now I need to talk to your guests and some of the guys who live in the bunkhouse. Maybe somebody saw something suspicious that can help us out."

"Good. Let me know if you find out anything." Dean glanced toward the house. "Are you going to be around awhile?"

"I can be," Ben answered. "Do you need something?"

"No. I have to go talk to Gwen. She's waiting in the office. I don't know how long it'll take. If you're gone when I come back, I'll give you a call in the morning."

An I-told-you-so grin pulled at Ben's mouth, and he gave a low chuckle. "Taking my advice, are you?"

Dean felt his face grow warm. "I don't know what's going to happen, but I have to find out if there's a chance for us."

His friend slapped him on the back. "Well, good luck. Let me know what she says."

Dean cast one last glance at his burning barn before he turned and started walking toward the house. At any other time the loss of a barn might have devastated him. But not tonight. Everybody was safe, and he was thankful for that, and now he was about to face what might very well be the worst blow of his life.

He entered the house through the door to the kitchen and stopped in the middle of the room. His heart was beating like a bass drum, and he could almost taste fear in his mouth. What if she said no to him? What would he do?

He closed his eyes for a moment. *Dear God,* he prayed, *I'm afraid. I love her so much, but I sense she has misgivings. I've told her how I feel. Now I*

pray for courage to hear her out. And then give me
the strength to accept and live in peace with what-
ever she has to say. Amen.

He opened his eyes and took a deep breath. Now to
face Gwen. He strode through the kitchen and down
the hall to the office. He stopped at the door before
entering and stared at her. She stood at the window,
her arms crossed over her chest, gazing out at the
burning barn. For a moment he stood still, enjoying
the pleasure that rippled through him at having her
here in his home.

"Gwen," he said softly, loving the way her name
sounded on his lips.

She turned slowly, dropped her arms to her sides
and leaned back against the windowsill. Her eyes
sparkled in the overhead light, and the sight of tears
caused his heart to race. Neither of them spoke as he
took a step toward her.

Then, before he knew what was happening, she ran
across the room, straight toward him. He grabbed her
in a fierce embrace, and her arms circled his neck.
His heart pumped even faster as she ran her fingers
into his hair and pulled his head toward hers. His lips
crushed down on hers, and he groaned as he tightened his hold on her.

He'd been longing for this moment for years, and
here it was. He was pouring all his hurt and grief from
the past into that one kiss, and she was answering
with the same emotion. In that instant he knew the
truth: she loved him as much as he loved her.

He pulled his head back and stared down at her.

"Gwen, I love you. I need you. Please tell me this means you're going to stay."

Tears streamed from her eyes as she tugged free of his arms. She turned and walked to the middle of the room, where she stopped and wiped her cheeks. He stood there, stunned, staring at her back. The way she'd kissed him had filled him with hope. Now he wasn't so sure.

Finally, she turned to face him. "I do love you, Dean. I want to stay more than I've ever wanted anything. But I can't." He took a step toward her, but she held out a hand to stop him. "Don't come any nearer," she said.

He felt as if the breath had been sucked from his body. "I don't understand. You love me, but you can't stay? It doesn't make sense. Why can't you? Is it Rick? Are you determined to marry him?"

Her forehead wrinkled, and she frowned. "Rick? No. I told you we were just good friends. I'm not in love with him."

Dean gritted his teeth and took another step toward her. "Then tell me why you kissed me."

She cringed back as if she couldn't bear for him to come a step closer. "Because I wanted one last kiss from you while you still think you love me. After I tell you what I must, you're going to hate me."

He shook his head. "I could never hate you, Gwen. I'll always love you."

"I wish that were true."

Now he was getting scared. He'd never seen such a look of agony on anyone's face. He took another step toward her, and she backed up until she was against the desk. He advanced and grabbed her hands. "Whatever you have to tell me, we can work it out together. What is it?"

She pulled one hand free, reached up and cupped his jaw. "I love you so much, Dean. And I've been so cruel and kept a secret from you that could have been the biggest blessing of your life. I'm so sorry. I only hope someday you can forgive me."

Her body shook so hard he thought she was going to collapse, and he slipped an arm around her waist and pulled her close, so close he could feel her breath on his face. "Tell me, Gwen," he muttered through clenched teeth. "What is it?"

She licked her lips and stared up at him. "I was pregnant when we divorced. We have a daughter."

TEN

For a moment she didn't know if Dean had heard her or not. He didn't breathe or move. He just stared at her. Then slowly he released her and took a step back. He swallowed, and his Adam's apple bobbed.

"What did you say?" he rasped.

He looked at her as if she was a total stranger, and Gwen realized that was exactly what she had just become to him. A stranger. Someone he didn't understand at all. She wanted to soothe the hurt she saw filling his eyes, but didn't know how.

"You have a daughter, Dean."

He closed his eyes for a brief moment and then opened them again. The hurt was still there. Perhaps it was more than hurt. Maybe it was already turning to hatred. She had to finish this while she could, and then she had to get out of here.

"Why?" he whispered. "Why would you keep that from me?"

"Because I was scared. You were drinking so much, and you'd become violent. You almost killed me."

His face turned ashen, and his lips trembled. "I never meant to hurt you."

"I know you didn't. It was the alcohol and the nightmares, but you did hurt me. I was afraid of what you might do to our child if she happened to be the one you attacked the next time you had one of your episodes—or if you attacked me again, while I was still pregnant. At the time I didn't think I could take a chance with her life."

"But it's been five years. During that time did it never occur to you to find out if I was still drinking? To check and see if I could be a father to my daughter?"

"I thought it was better if I didn't know. And I couldn't risk letting you find out about her if you were still drinking."

He turned and stumbled across the room to the window, where he grabbed hold of the sill to steady himself. He didn't speak for a few moments, just stared outside. Then he spoke in a soft voice. "What's her name?"

"Maggie."

"Maggie," he repeated. "I like that. What does she look like?"

A tear rolled down Gwen's cheek. "She has your eyes and my hair. She has a dimple in her chin and a strawberry birthmark on her shoulder just like yours." Gwen picked up the framed photo she'd laid face-down on the desk before Dean came in from the barn. "Here's a picture of her."

He reached for it, and his hand trembled as he

pulled it to him. His gaze raked the photograph for several minutes, and then he began to trace Maggie's face on the glass with his index finger. "I thought I had nobody. And all that time I had…" The words ended on a sob, and he wiped his eyes. He cleared his throat and tried to speak again. "Does she go to school?"

"She started preschool this year, and her teacher says she's very smart. She's already reading, and she's a wonderful artist. She's always drawing me pictures. Our refrigerator is covered with them all the time."

"I've never had the opportunity to hang them on my fridge."

The accusation cut deep, and the sorrow in his eyes even deeper. "I'm so sorry, Dean. I know now how wrong it was, but at the time it seemed the only thing to do."

He held up the picture. "May I keep this?"

"Of course. And I'll make sure you have current photos from now on."

He took a deep breath and glared at her. "I don't think I'll be satisfied with pictures. I want to see her. I want to go to New York and spend time with her so I can get to know her. Then I want her here at my house for visits. She won't get to meet my grandfather now, but at least she can see the house and the land he loved."

"Of course. I'll give you our address and the name and address of my lawyer before I leave in the morning. You can have yours get in touch with mine, and we'll work out a custody agreement. Is that okay with you?"

He looked down at the picture he held and nodded. "That will be fine with me."

She swallowed the lump in her throat. "Then I'll leave first thing in the morning."

"I'll be in touch," he said.

The curt dismissal felt like a punch in the stomach, and Gwen ran after him as he headed toward the door. She grabbed him by the arm, and he stopped, but didn't look at her, just stared straight ahead. "Dean, I understand how you must feel about me right now, but I want you to know I meant it when I said I love you. I hope someday you can forgive me."

There was only a small tremor in his cheek that gave any indication her words had reached him. Then he sighed and bit down on his lip. "I hope so, too, Gwen."

With that, he pulled free from her and walked from the office. A few minutes later she heard the kitchen door bang shut, and she ran to the window and peered outside. She watched as Dean walked across the backyard, which was still lit by flames at the barn. His shoulders were slumped, and he didn't look back. A group of ranch hands stood to one side in the shadows. He walked into their midst and was swallowed up by the night.

Sobbing, Gwen rushed from the office and upstairs to her room. She flung herself on her bed and buried her face in the pillow as she cried out her misery.

She'd known that he would hate her, but she hadn't thought it would hurt this much.

There was no way she could survive an encounter with Dean in the morning. She'd leave him the information she'd promised on his desk and be out of here before the sun was up.

Dean tried to concentrate on the ranch hands' conversation going on around him, but couldn't. All he could think about was the face of that little girl in the photograph. His daughter. A daughter he didn't know he had. How could Gwen do something to him like that?

She'd certainly had him fooled. All the time she'd been here, she'd been hiding this secret. Maybe he'd never really known her at all.

He walked away from the circle of men and moved closer to the barn. The firemen were still working to get the fire under control; apparently, it was proving more difficult than they'd thought. The flame-retardant paint had kept the blaze from spreading quickly, but since individual fires had been set all over the barn, the fire had still got into everything. It looked as if when it was finally extinguished he'd have nothing left but a pile of ashes.

That had little consequence for him at the moment. He'd always thought possessions were important, but tonight he'd found out differently. He would give every penny he had if he could just get those lost years back, if he could go back and erase the drinking from his life. If he could do that, he might have had Maggie all along. But he hadn't, and Gwen hadn't even considered letting him know. Well, now he knew. The only question that remained was what he was going to do about it.

"Are you okay, Dean?"

Startled by the voice beside him, he whirled, to find Billy standing there. Dean exhaled a deep breath and nodded. "Yeah, I'm okay, thanks. It's just been a wild few days."

"I know," Billy said. They stood in silence for a moment as they stared at the barn. "Looks like the roof will cave in anytime now."

Dean didn't reply, just stared into the flames. After a few minutes he turned to his neighbor. "Thanks for being here tonight."

"Glad to do it. I'm just glad I could help get those puppies out. When I saw Gwen run into that barn, I thought I was going to have a heart attack. She could have been killed."

"I know. She acted without thinking, and it could have ended very differently."

Billy glanced around at the people still gathered at the scene. "Where is she, by the way? I thought I saw her here not too long ago."

"She's in her room. Packing, I guess. She's leaving first thing in the morning."

"Leaving? Why is she leaving?"

Dean shrugged. "She needs to get back to New York."

"But—but I thought…" He paused.

Dean turned his head and stared at him. "What did you think?"

Billy shifted from one foot to the other as if he had suddenly become embarrassed about what he was going to say. "I thought…well, I thought the two of you might get back together, and she would stay on. I know James kept hoping that would happen someday."

Dean exhaled a deep breath and stuck his hands in his pockets. "So did I, but it doesn't look like that's to be."

"I'm sorry, Dean. Maybe something will happen that will reunite the two of you."

"Don't hold your breath, Billy."

Ben walked up just then and frowned when he saw Dean's face. "What's wrong? You look like you've just lost your best friend."

He stared back, unblinking. "Maybe I have. It didn't work out. Gwen's leaving first thing in the morning."

Ben's mouth opened, but he didn't say anything. Then he nodded. "Sorry about that. Things could change. Don't give up."

"That's what I was just telling him," Billy said.

Dean shook his head. "I know you guys mean well, but I think it's too late for that. But don't worry about me. I'll be okay. I just need to get away and think for a while."

"Then I'll get out of here and leave you alone," Billy said. "If you need me for anything, let me know."

Dean clapped him on the shoulder. "I will, and thanks again, Billy."

When he'd driven away, Ben turned back to Dean. "You sure you're going to be okay?"

He smiled and gave his friend a playful punch in the arm. "Don't worry. I'm not going to do anything stupid to disappoint my sponsor, like going out and getting drunk. I've come too far for that. I may not have Gwen, but I have something else to live for. I just found out that I have a daughter."

Ben's eyes grew wide, and his mouth gaped open. "You have a daughter?"

"Yeah. Gwen was pregnant when we got a divorce, and she never told me about the baby. She says she was trying to protect her from the man I'd become."

Ben propped his hands on his hips and shook his head. "Then that explains why she made you promise not to look for her. She didn't want you to find out about your child."

"Well, I know now, and I intend to meet Maggie and have a relationship with her. She needs to know she has a father."

Ben's eyes crinkled at the corners as he smiled. "And a good one now. But back then…"

Dean arched his eyebrows. "What are you saying?"

"From what you've told me, and the way you were when you came here, I don't think you could have been a father then."

The memory of those years washed over him, and he nodded. "You're right. But it's been five years, and she never even tried to find out if I was okay or not."

Ben pursed his lips and stared at the burning barn again. "Yeah, five years of you telling me how much you love her and that you wanted her back no matter what. How do you feel about Gwen now?"

Dean exhaled and rubbed the back of his neck. "That's a good question. I really don't know."

"Then that's something you have to figure out. I only met Gwen yesterday, but she doesn't strike me as the kind of person who would be vindictive. What if she's telling the truth, and only wanted to protect herself and her child from the horror of living with an alcoholic?" Ben put his hand on Dean's shoulder and squeezed. "So let your old sponsor give you another piece of advice, friend. Don't do anything rash. Think about it, and ask God what He wants you to do. You'll know what the best decision is."

"You're right—what I really need is to spend time with God. I usually get on Midnight and ride up to Crystal Falls, but I guess I can't do that tonight. My saddle probably burned with all the others in the barn. So I guess I'll have to find another place to go."

"Well, one thing's for sure," Ben said. "God already knows about it. All you have to do is find a quiet place and sit still so you can let Him help you decide what's the best route for you to take. If Gwen's planning on leaving, I'd suggest you get on this right away."

Dean smiled wryly. "Ben, I wish I had your confidence. You seem happy all the time, and you always know the right thing to do."

He let out a snort. "Don't be fooled, buddy. We all have problems. Some people don't like to talk about them."

Dean tilted his head and gazed at him. "Maybe someday you'll share them with me."

His friend exhaled. "Maybe I will. But for now, get out of here and decide what to do before Gwen takes off."

"You're right. I'll go check with the fire chief to see how long they think they'll be. Then I think I'll walk down to the pond in the field back of the barn. It was always one of Granddad's favorite places to go be alone."

"Then I'm gonna head back to the office and check the records for your phone. Maybe the provider can tell me something about where that text you received came from. I'll call as soon as I know anything."

Ben turned and walked toward his squad car. Dean watched him go and then shifted his gaze to the upstairs window of the room where Gwen was staying. Even though the curtains had been drawn, the light shone through. He wondered what she was doing right now. Then the light went out, and he pressed his lips together. If she was already going to bed, she must not have been as bothered by their conversation as he was. Maybe that was because she'd known for five years they had a daughter, and he'd found out about it less than an hour ago.

He rubbed his hands over his eyes. There was nothing he could do about the past five years, but he could choose the path he wanted to take for the future. Now all he had to do was decide what that was.

The fire chief was staring at the dying blaze when Dean walked over to him. "How's it going, Keith?"

"It's dying down, but we'll be here until we think it's fully extinguished. Then we'll come back in the morning, when it's cooled off some, and start our investigation. There's no need for you to hang around here. No one was hurt, and the horses are safe. So go on and get some rest."

Dean shook his head. "I don't think I'll be able to sleep any tonight. But I will be leaving you to it, since I've got something I need to do. I'll see you before you go."

He turned, glanced at Gwen's dark window once again and walked to the corral. He leaned on the fence for a moment and said a prayer of thanks that the horses had all been saved, then headed across the field.

The small pond that he'd fished in ever since he was a boy lay at the back. Dying flames still lit the area as he trudged toward it and the wooden bench on the bank where his grandfather had spent so many hours.

The clouds had cleared, and moonlight sparkled on the quiet water. If it wasn't for the fire's glow and the occasional sound of a fireman's voice in the still night, he would have thought he was alone. He gazed up at the stars, which suddenly seemed brighter than they ever had, and he knew he wasn't alone.

A weariness spread through his body, and Dean leaned forward with his elbows on his knees and buried his face in his hands. He'd been so happy when Gwen had reappeared in his life, but a short while ago she had stolen all that joy. Now he had a decision to make. He either had to forgive her or decide to hate her forever. Either way, he intended to be a part of his daughter's life.

He looked up at the stars one more time, fell to his knees and bowed his head. "God, help me," he begged. "Show me what to do."

ELEVEN

The sun had just come up when Gwen carried her suitcases downstairs, set them in the entry hall and stopped outside the office. The door stood open, but Dean wasn't in there. She walked to the window and looked toward the barn. A few firemen still stood beside the smoldering remains of what had once been a beautiful barn, but Dean was nowhere to be seen. Maybe he had finally come inside and was asleep right now.

It was just as well. She didn't want to see him anyway.

She pulled the letter she'd written before she went to bed last night from her purse and laid it on the desk in a spot where he'd see it right away. She'd put his name on it so that anyone else working in the office this morning wouldn't open it. She supposed this room would be quite busy when the guests awoke and people began checking out. With any luck she'd be almost to Knoxville by then.

She stepped back into the hall, picked up her bags and looked around the house that held such happy memories for her—visiting Dean's grandfather in the summers, coming here on holidays. For a brief second last night, she had thought maybe she and Dean could recapture that time and build a life together with their daughter. He had killed that hope when he'd walked away from her. Now all they could do was attempt to be civil as they coordinated joint custody of their daughter.

Holding her head high, Gwen walked out the front door and down the steps to her car. Within minutes she'd stowed her bags in the back and was on her way down the driveway to the main road. There shouldn't be much traffic this time of morning, and if all went well, she could have the rental returned and be checked in at the airport in plenty of time for her flight.

She yawned and tried to shake the sluggish feeling from her head. Maybe she should have got a cup of coffee before she left. After her conversation with Dean last night, she hadn't been able to sleep, and this morning she ached from head to toe with exhaustion. She only hoped the flight to New York was a smooth one, because she intended to sleep all the way there.

At the moment, though, she needed to concentrate on the winding road that led from the ranch into town. Living in New York, she had little use for a car and depended on public transportation. She was out of practice driving at all, much less around such sharp curves.

Ahead, she spotted an especially tricky stretch, with two hairpin curves that always took her breath away. The road twisted in 180-degree turns, one after the other, requiring a driver to brake sharply in order to navigate the switchbacks. Gwen bit her lip, slowed the car and watched for oncoming traffic as she made the first curve.

At the end of the second one, the road entered a tunnel through the side of the mountain. As she pulled into it, she smiled and couldn't resist honking the horn, as she and Dean used to do when they'd traveled this road.

The blare of the horn echoed off the walls, but her smile quickly changed to a frown when the car engine sputtered and died about halfway through the tunnel. As the vehicle glided to a stop, she glanced down at the gas gauge, but it registered half-full. Looking under the hood for the cause of the breakdown would do no good, for Gwen had no idea of the names of the parts underneath or their functions, much less how to fix them if they broke.

She reached for her purse to get out her cell phone and then remembered it likely still lay at the bottom of Rattlesnake Creek. Her only hope for help was for someone to come by and stop. This wasn't a well-traveled road, though, and it could be a while before anyone happened upon her.

Mentally, she calculated the distance into Gatlinburg, the nearest place where she could get a ride. She had to be at least three miles away. The thought of walking that distance pulling two suitcases didn't appeal to her, but she didn't seem to have much choice.

Gwen pulled the keys from the ignition and grabbed her purse before she stepped out of the car and walked around to the back. The keyhole for the trunk was barely visible in the tunnel's dim lights, but she managed to insert the key and pop the lid. She had just reached inside to retrieve her suitcases when she heard the sound of an approaching vehicle. Turning to stare in that direction, she spied a battered Jeep approaching. It pulled up beside her, the driver's door opened and Billy Champion stepped out.

"Gwen," he said in surprise. "What are you doing out here this early in the morning?"

She gave a sigh of relief. "I'm on my way to the airport at Knoxville, and my car broke down. I'm so glad to see you. Can you give me a lift to the nearest garage so I can get someone to come tow it in for me?"

"Sure I can. Did you rent this car in Gatlinburg?"

"No, I got it in Knoxville, but if I can get it to a garage, then I can call the rental company and have them send someone over to pick it up. I'll have to find a way to the airport, though."

Billy smiled and walked toward her. "Then it's a good thing I came by. I'm on my way to Knoxville, and I can drop you at the airport. Let's get your bags."

She pulled the key from the trunk and nodded. "I'd appreciate a ride." Gwen was about to grab the handle of her larger suitcase when she spotted a pair of shoes lying at the back of the trunk. She'd worn them on one of her first visits to a possible location and had thrown them inside afterward. She would need those shoes when she got home, and she bent over farther to reach them so she could stuff them in her suitcase.

"I haven't had any problem with this car all the

time I've had it. I can't imagine what could be wrong with it," she said as she unzipped one of the bags and slipped the shoes inside.

Billy stepped up closer behind her. "It could be a kill switch," he said. "They'll stop a car before you know what's happening."

She'd never heard of such a thing, but then, she knew little about what went on under the hood. "A kill switch, huh?" she muttered absently. "Is that something new on cars now?"

"Yeah, kinda new," he said. "Lending companies sometimes put them on cars they finance for customers with bad credit. That way if they don't receive payment, they can stop a car anywhere they want, even on a highway, repossess it right there and leave the driver stranded."

"Well, I don't know why the rental company would put one on this car. My credit is great. I'll speak to them about this. In the meantime, I'm glad you came by. You're a lifesaver. I don't know—"

She stopped midsentence when she felt a sharp prick in her neck. She pressed her hand to the spot, which felt as if it had been stung by a bee, and turned to stare in disbelief at Billy, who stood there holding a hypodermic needle in his hand. A smile pulled at his lips, and he grabbed her arm as she stumbled back against the car.

"What was that?" She knew that was her voice speaking, but somehow it sounded slurred.

"First of all," he said, "the rental company didn't put that switch on your car. I did. The first night you came to the ranch. I just had to wait for the right moment to use it. And second, I'm not a lifesaver. Quite the opposite."

A dizzy feeling assaulted her, and she felt her knees grow weak. She put out a hand to steady herself, attempting to brace it against the car. "What did you give me?"

"Just a little something to help you relax," he said. "In a minute you won't feel a thing."

The car keys she held and the purse hanging on her shoulder slipped to the ground. Gwen tried to grab for them, but it was no use. She blinked and tried to refocus on Billy's face. It wavered and rippled in her vision, and the leering look he directed at her sent chills down her spine. With a desperate groan, she tried to force her shaking legs to straighten, but failed. She was drifting toward unconsciousness, and there wasn't anything she could do about it.

She opened her mouth to scream, but no sound came out. Billy was right. She couldn't feel anything.

Dean skipped another rock across the quiet pond and glanced up at the sunrise just beginning to break. He loved this time of day in the mountains. To him, the red-and-yellow-streaked sky, along with the blue haze from the mountaintops, sent a message from God that this was indeed the day that He had made.

Today that message was received loud and clear. This was not a day to be wasted. Dean had a decision to make, and so far he had no idea what it was going to be. He'd struggled all night as he'd sat on the bench beside the pond and wrestled with the question of what he wanted to do about Gwen.

As the night had worn on, he had come to the conclusion that he had two choices. The first one was to contact his lawyer and begin the process of trying to work out some kind of custody agreement with Gwen.

He picked up another rock and threw it with all his might into the pond, where it hit with a splash and sent small waves rippling outward. A custody agreement wasn't going to get back the years he'd lost with his daughter.

The second option he had was to forgive her. He chuckled to himself at how easily he'd given that advice to others in the past. He'd always counseled people to let go of their anger and their grudges. Well, now he knew firsthand that forgiving was a lot harder than he'd ever thought. It meant he would have to quit thinking of himself as a wronged person and would have to sacrifice his hurt feelings. But the potential reward would be enormous, since only through forgiveness would he have a chance at a restored relationship with Gwen.

When he weighed the two options in his mind and debated which would be the best for his daughter, he knew the answer. Of course it would be better for her if he and Gwen could have a good and loving relationship.

That might be best for Maggie. But what about him? Didn't he deserve to get some kind of victory over Gwen for what she'd done to him?

Dean stood and began to pace up and down the bank of the pond. He'd been so hopeful last night in the office when she'd run to him and kissed him and told him she loved him. He'd been so happy for one short minute, until she made her confession to him.

Why had God let this happen to him? Dean had stopped in the kitchen on the way to the office and prayed that...

He halted in his pacing now and swallowed the sick feeling coming from his stomach. His prayer. He'd forgotten about that. What was it he'd asked God to do? And then his words rose up in his mind: *give me the strength to accept and live in peace with whatever she has to say*, he'd prayed.

Dean staggered back to the bench where he'd sat with his grandfather so many times and sank down on it. He'd had the answer all along, before he even came out here. And the words had come from his own mouth. He had to forgive her.

Suddenly he realized the truth. If he'd been a different person five years ago, he would have had his daughter from the start. But he'd been an alcoholic who'd put his wife's life in danger, and there was no way he could have been a good father. He and Gwen both had made mistakes that had affected their daughter's life. But those mistakes didn't have to determine their future. Now they had a chance to lay the past to rest—to start to forgive each other and find out if there was any way the three of them could be a family.

He turned and ran back to the house as fast as he could. When he burst through the back door, Shorty gave a startled shout. "Dean, you scared me to death. What's the matter?"

"Gwen," he panted. "Has she come down for breakfast yet?"

"No, not yet. I figured she was sleeping in after the night we had."

Dean walked over to the coffeepot and poured himself a cup. "It was a hard night. I'll let her sleep in. Let me know when she wakes up. I'll be in the office."

Holding his coffee, he headed that direction. When he entered the room, he went to the window and stood there sipping his coffee and gazing out at the three firemen who still watched the smoldering remains of his barn. Those guys had to be tired. He'd have to ask Shorty to get them some breakfast.

Dean was about to turn to do that when his cell phone rang. He pulled it out of his pocket and saw Ben's name on caller ID. "Good morning, Ben."

"Morning," he replied. "I've been up all night, but I'm on my way home to get some sleep and thought I'd let you know I got some information from the phone company about the text you received."

Dean's back straightened, and he gripped the phone tighter. "And?"

"Like I thought, it was a burner phone. So no record of who it belongs to, but I did find out one interesting fact."

"What's that?"

"The tower the cell phone hit when it relayed the message is the same one that yours did, the tower just down the road from your ranch."

Dean set his coffee cup on the table next to the window and rubbed his hand across his eyes. "Oh, man. That means whoever texted me was close enough to see the fire."

"That's right. In fact, he could have been standing at your ranch setting the fire when he texted."

"And he could even have been here with me watching it burn."

"That's just speculation, but you could be right. Anyway, I wanted to give you this information before I checked out for a few hours. If anything else turns up, I'll let you know."

"Thanks, Ben."

There was a brief pause before his friend spoke again. "How are you this morning? Have you come to any decision yet?"

Dean smiled. "Yes. Gwen's still sleeping, but when she wakes up, I intend to talk to her. I think we both have things to forgive each other for. I love Gwen, and I want to get to know my daughter. We need to be together, all three of us." His throat closed up, and he cleared it. "I want my family, Ben."

Ben's laughter drifted into his ear. "Good choice, buddy. I'll be praying that it's gonna work out for you. Have a good day."

"I plan to."

Dean ended the call and stood there smiling for a few moments as he thought of all the things he wanted to say to Gwen. Then he exhaled a deep breath. For now, though, he needed to get to work. This was going to be a busy morning, with guests leaving and him having to cancel all the upcoming reservations.

He turned back toward the desk and spotted an envelope lying there. Frowning, he walked over and picked it up. The sight of his name written in Gwen's precise handwriting made his heart drop to the pit of his stomach. Dean tore the envelope open. The note contained only a few short lines.

Dear Dean,
Please believe me when I say I'm sorry for keeping the truth from you. I will always love you no matter how you feel about me. Enclosed is my card. Please have your lawyer get in contact with me about arranging for shared custody, and I will agree to anything you ask. I think that's only fair.
Goodbye,
Gwen.

The letter and card fluttered from his hands and landed on the desk. He couldn't believe what he'd read. She was gone? Without even giving them a chance to try to figure out what they should do?

No, he couldn't let this happen. He had to find her and bring her back so they could talk.

He barreled from the room and out the front door. His truck sat beside the house, and he jumped in, then roared down the driveway toward the main road. He had no idea how long she'd been gone or how far she could have got, but it didn't matter. He would find her. He would follow her all the way to New York if need be.

He wanted his family back, and if any part of Gwen wanted that, too, then he wouldn't allow anything to stop them from having it.

TWELVE

Gwen struggled to open her eyes, but it seemed to be too much of an ordeal. All she wanted to do was sleep, but she couldn't. She felt certain she had something she needed to do, but at the moment couldn't think what that might be. Still, she had to make herself open her eyes.

"I see you're about to come back to life."

The voice startled her, and her body trembled. Her eyes popped open, and she stared upward into bright lights. She tried to move, but her limbs wouldn't respond. Slowly, her hazy thoughts began to clear, and she stiffened in surprise when she realized she was sitting in a chair with her hands tied behind her back. She struggled to get free, but it was no use. She was tied too tightly.

Fear shot through her as the memory returned of Billy stopping to help her and a needle prick. She wriggled again in the seat, but couldn't loosen her hands. She stilled for a moment, and then a new fear shot through her. Where was she, and what was going to happen to her?

Cold sweat poured down her face, and her lips and chin quivered as she slowly turned her head and took in her surroundings. Her eyes grew wide as she realized she sat in the middle of a rodeo arena. Not just any arena, but one she had been to years ago with Dean. Lambert's Practice Arena, where riders honed their skills for rodeo competition.

Livestock panels perhaps six or seven feet high fenced the area, and at either end she could see chutes for holding animals before they were released into the ring. As she stared at the chute at the far end, the gate shook, and a loud thumping sound sent a chill through her. What was behind that gate?

"Renegade's restless today," a voice behind her said.

She tried to turn her head to see the speaker, but it was no use. She sensed movement beside her, and then Billy Champion stepped into view. He grinned at her, but it wasn't in a friendly manner. The man who had seemed so sympathetic to her plight when he stopped to assist her now looked as if he was possessed with pure evil.

Her breath hitched in her throat, and she swallowed. "Why have you brought me to Lambert's Arena, Billy? And where is everybody?"

"I brought you here so we could have some quiet time together, Gwen. We don't have to worry about being interrupted, because the arena's closed. That means all the employees are off enjoying being with their families except me. Mr. Lambert was so appreciative, when I started working here, that I was willing to come in alone to feed the livestock when everybody else was off." He shrugged. "Of course, I didn't mind, because I don't have a family."

The chute rattled again, and she nodded in that direction. "You said Renegade is restless. What's behind that gate?"

Billy laughed. "An old friend of mine. Renegade is a bull, the one all the cowboys hope to beat. He's a mean one, all right, one of the worst I've ever seen. And I've seen a lot of them."

"You're making no sense. Please tell me what's going on here."

A wistful smile pulled at Billy's mouth. "Years ago I was a stock contractor for rodeos. I had the reputation of having some of the toughest stock in the business, and all the big rodeos wanted to use my animals. Of course, they didn't know that I was in partnership with a breeder down in Mexico who used some *special* methods to produce bucking animals that were almost impossible to ride. We had a scheme in place to smuggle our horses and bulls into the country and produce false papers that said they'd been bred in the States."

"But that's illegal. How did you think you could get away with it?"

He shrugged. "I was young and foolish. I wasn't afraid to take some chances. In the long run, though, it didn't pay off. We got caught, and I spent the next twenty years in jail. My son was just six years old when I went to prison, and when I got out, he was dead."

Gwen's heart thudded in her chest as she stared

up at him. "Billy, I'm sorry about that, but it doesn't explain why you're doing this." A menacing snarl was her only answer as he turned and started to walk away. "Billy! I don't understand!"

He whirled and stormed back to her, his fists clenched at his sides and a deadly rage etched into his face. "I didn't understand, either, when Dean killed my son."

Gwen wanted to shrink away from him as he came nearer, but that was impossible. Instead, she tried to swallow back the fear that was quickly taking over her body and stared up at him. "What are you talking about?"

Her captor bent forward again, until his face was only a few inches from hers. "My son, Trip King. Dean killed him."

Her eyes grew wide again, and she flinched at the fury he directed toward her. "Your son? How can that be? Your name is Billy Champion."

He gave a snort and shook his head. "That's what I told everybody, but it's not. My real name is King. Aaron King, and I'm Trip King's father."

"But…but I don't get it. I thought Trip's father was dead."

Aaron laughed. "My wife divorced me when I was sent to prison and told everybody that I was dead. But I wasn't. I had a son, and I kept up with him all his life. He was going to be somebody, the only thing I had in my life to be proud of. A world champion bull rider and maybe a movie star. Everyone was going to know his name. But he never got his chance." Aaron leaned forward again and yelled into her face, "Because Dean killed him! That's why he has to pay!"

Gwen tried to process what he was saying. "So you're after revenge?"

"Yes!" He raked his hand through his hair and began to pace up and down in front of her.

"I don't understand," she said. "Trip's death happened years ago. If you wanted to get even with Dean, why have you waited so long?"

"Because I didn't get out of jail until a year ago. When I did, I changed my name, came here and rented that house on the Little Pigeon Ranch. I worked at becoming friends with Dean and his grandfather, and I studied them while I planned on how I was going to repay Dean for what he did."

"But his grandfather liked you. He trusted you, helped you get a job with the Lamberts."

"Yeah, he did. Am I supposed to feel grateful for that, after what Dean did to me? All that time I was just waiting for the right moment to strike—to hurt him like he'd hurt me. And then it came."

The man's eyes darkened with burning hatred, and Gwen cringed from the heat of his glare. "What do you mean?"

Aaron stopped pacing and came back to stand in front of her. "I decided it wasn't enough just to kill Dean. I had to make him suffer, too. So I invited James to go hiking with me the other day. We did that a lot. And when we were on the trail, with him leading the way, it was easy to hit him on the head with a rock I'd picked up."

She gasped. "You were the one I saw dumping his body in the stream?"

He nodded. "Yeah. When I saw you, I didn't know if you'd seen me kill him or not. But I knew I had to stop you from going to the authorities. I thought I had, but from where I was hiding in the woods I saw them put you in the ambulance. So I had to try again."

"You shot at the ambulance and made us crash?"

Aaron chuckled. "Yeah, and I don't mind telling you when I opened that ambulance door after the wreck, I was surprised to see Dean with you. I thought I'd better get out of there before he recognized me. But I had a bigger surprise when he brought you home and I recognized you from James's picture as Dean's ex-wife. That's when I decided I could hurt him a bit more by killing you, too. The barn was just something I threw in after I botched the ambush at Rattle-snake Creek."

"That was you, too?"

"Guilty as charged," he said with a laugh.

"B-but you helped me with the puppies. Why did you do that?"

Aaron placed his hand over his heart and stared up at the ceiling. "Just being a good neighbor who wanted to help out a friend." He dropped his arm to his side and glared at her. "And it worked. Dean was so grateful to me for helping keep you safe. It'll never occur to him to doubt or question me until it's too late."

Gwen sucked in a breath to try to slow her racing heart. Although she wanted to yell back at him, it was clear that would do no good. She needed to remain calm and try to reason with him, though she had her doubts that would prove successful. He was already so agitated he looked as if he might explode any minute.

"Billy—" she began.

"Aaron!" he interrupted. "You can call me Aaron now. It's not as if you're ever going to tell anybody."

His words sent a new wave of fear rushing through her, but she tried not to show how she'd been affected. "All right, Aaron. Think about what you're saying. We all agree that Trip's death was a terrible thing. I know Dean has suffered from guilt ever since it happened, but we can't change the past."

The man's face turned bright red, and a spot of saliva seeped from the corner of his mouth. "He should suffer. He killed my son. Shot him down in cold blood."

"No, you're wrong, Aaron. Please think about what you're saying. Dean was a police officer. Your son was a drug dealer, and he killed another policeman. Instead of dropping his gun when Dean ordered him to, Trip aimed it at him. Dean didn't have a choice. The investigation proved that it was self-defense."

"Lies! All of it lies!" her captor shouted. "The police covered up Trip's murder and took care of their own. Dean may have gotten away with it then, but he's not going to now."

"Billy—I mean, Aaron—Dean didn't want to shoot your son, but Trip gave him no choice."

"Well, I have a choice, and I'm taking it right now," he spit as he pulled his cell phone from his pocket.

"Say cheese," he said and snapped her picture. Then he held it up for her to see.

Gwen's stomach churned at the way she appeared in the photograph. Her tousled hair looked as if it hadn't been combed in days, and her bloodshot eyes gave evidence of her sleepless night. But it was the expression of pure fright on her face that made her heart race. Anyone looking at the picture would know right away that she was terrified.

She turned her gaze on Aaron. "What are you going to do with that picture?"

Busy tapping out a text message, he only smiled. When he'd finished, he took a deep breath. "Now all we have to do is wait for Dean to get here."

He turned and started to walk away, but Gwen called out to him. "Aaron, why did you text Dean?"

He stopped and stood still for a moment before he sauntered back to where she sat. "I thought he might like to try to save his wife, so I've invited him to the party. Of course, he won't be able to change things. Not with Renegade in the ring with you." Aaron tilted his head to one side and grinned. "Did you know that bulls are very unpredictable? In fact, only one person in twenty survives an attack by a bull."

Gwen's heart leaped into her throat, and she began to shake. "What do you mean to do?"

"Well," he said, "I'm going now to get Renegade ready to meet you and Dean. I don't think that meeting will turn out well for either of you. Of course, one of you could be the one in twenty that survives, but it seems far more likely you'll both be among the other nineteen."

Gwen cast a quick glance toward where Renegade snorted and bucked against the railings. "You wouldn't..."

"Oh, yes, I would." Her captor leaned close to her. "Bulls are the most dangerous livestock animals to be around, Gwen. From a standing-still position, they can turn on a dime and outrun a human. Once he attacks he will either gore a person to death or crush them. I wonder which it will be with you."

"Aaron, please," Gwen begged. "This is insane. You have to let me go."

"I don't have to do anything I don't want to." His eyes narrowed into sinister slits. "Right now the one thing I want to do is get Renegade ready to meet you."

"Wh-what are you going t-to do?"

"A little trick I learned when I was a livestock contractor. If you've ever seen a bull-riding event, you'll know the bull has a flank strap around it. The contractor has to make sure the strap is tight enough to stay on, but loose enough to make the bull think he can kick it off. A seventeen-hundred-pound bull sure can kick." Aaron held up a finger as if to emphasize a point. "But if the contractor wants the bull to *really* kick, he can insert some kind of sharp objects under the strap. That drives them wild."

Gwen cast a terrified glance toward the chute that held Renegade. It rattled again, and the sharp tip of one of his horns appeared between the slats of the panel gate. She tried to look away, but the sight of that horn and the thought of how it could rip into a human body paralyzed her with fear. "P-please, Aaron, let me go!"

He shook his head. "Sorry. Can't do it, Gwen. I don't imagine it'll be too long before Dean gets here. That picture I sent him should do the trick. Now just sit still and be quiet or I might decide to silence you before I turn Renegade loose."

With that, he spun around and strode toward the chute. She started to call after him, to beg him to let her live for her daughter's sake. Then a terrifying thought flashed in her mind. If he found out she and Dean had a daughter, he might go after Maggie once they were dead. Gwen couldn't risk letting him know that.

She struggled against the bindings at her back but they didn't budge. There was no way she was going to escape. All she could do was wait for Aaron to do what he'd promised.

She closed her eyes, and a tear dripped down her cheek. Less than twelve hours ago she had been hoping that Dean would forgive her and that the three of them could be a family. Now she sat alone in the middle of a rodeo practice arena and waited for a killer to take his revenge.

God, take care of my little girl, she prayed as the tears continued to spill from her eyes.

Dean knew he was exceeding the speed limit on the road from the ranch into town, but he didn't have a choice. Every minute was crucial if he was to catch up with Gwen and stop her before she got on a plane. If the police caught him, he would gladly accept a ticket and pay the fine, if it meant he could reach her in time.

As he drove, he rehearsed what he was going to say to her. He would tell her that he loved her, that he would never love another woman. And that he wanted his family. Ideally, he wanted Gwen and Maggie with him at Little Pigeon Ranch, but he wasn't sure Gwen would want the same thing.

After all, she had a good job in New York and a home there. Maggie was used to her school and her friends. How would it affect her to be uprooted from all she'd ever known to move to a ranch in the Smoky Mountains and live with a father she'd never met? Those were questions to be answered later.

The important thing was for Gwen and him to accept that they had both made mistakes and needed to forgive each other. That would be the foundation for the life he wanted for them, for their family. First, though, he had to catch up with her and convince her to come back to the ranch so they could talk out their problems.

He slowed the truck in anticipation of the two hairpin curves just ahead. He'd driven this road hundreds of times and always slowed for these curves. But today of all days he had to make sure he navigated them perfectly. If he was to catch Gwen, he couldn't afford to lose control of the truck and end up at the bottom of the embankment.

As he came out of the second curve and entered the tunnel, his eyes grew wide at the sight of Gwen's rental, the trunk lid raised, stopped halfway through the passage. He stomped on the brakes, and the truck came to a skidding stop right behind the vehicle. Dean was out and running toward the parked sedan as soon as the engine died. The sight of Gwen's purse and car keys on the ground made him come to an abrupt halt, and his stomach clenched. Her suitcases were still in the trunk, but she was nowhere to be seen.

He ran to the front, yanked the door open and stared inside. Nothing seemed out of the ordinary. A further search of the car yielded no clues as to what had happened or where Gwen might have gone. Dean thrust his fingers through his hair. Where was she? She wouldn't have left on her own without her purse.

He pulled his phone from his pocket and dialed Ben's number. His friend answered after two rings, his voice hoarse as if he'd been awakened from sleep. "Hey, Dean, what—"

Dean didn't let him finish. "I just found Gwen's car abandoned in the tunnel past the two hairpin curves on the road into town. She's nowhere in sight, but her purse and keys are on the ground at the back of the car and her suitcases are still in the trunk. I'm afraid the killer got to her."

He heard a creaking sound and realized Ben had just sat up in bed. "I'll get some deputies out there right away, and I'll come, too."

"Good. I'll drive on toward town and see if I can

find any trace of her. Let me know if you find out anything."

"I will."

Dean disconnected the call, picked up Gwen's keys and purse, and ran back toward his truck. He'd just settled in the driver's seat when his phone chimed, indicating he had a new text. He opened the message and gasped at the picture that popped up.

Gwen sat in a chair, and it was evident that her hands were tied behind her back. But where was she? In the background he could see livestock panels. She had to be in an enclosed area used to corral animals. But where?

He glanced down at the text, and the hair on the back of his neck stood up. If you want to save Gwen, come to Lambert's Practice Arena. I don't think she'll last eight seconds in the ring with Renegade.

With shaking fingers, he punched Ben's number into his phone again. His friend answered right away. "Dean—"

"Ben," he yelled, "I just got a text with a picture of Gwen tied to a chair. He's got her at Lambert's Arena. He says he's going to turn Renegade loose on her."

Ben gasped. "Renegade? He's the meanest bull Lambert's got. He'll kill her."

"I know," Dean groaned as he turned the key in the ignition and then roared out of the tunnel. "I'm on my way there. Can you meet me?"

"As soon as possible, and I'll bring backup. I'm

at home, so I'm farther away than you are. If you get there before my deputies, be careful."

"I will. See you there."

Dean disconnected the call and pushed the accelerator almost to the floorboard. The truck surged forward, and he gripped the steering wheel tighter. He had to get to Gwen in time.

Fifteen minutes later he pulled to a stop in the gravel parking lot of Lambert's Practice Arena. The place looked deserted, and he remembered this was the one day a week the arena was closed. Whoever had brought Gwen here had to know that.

He reached over, opened the glove compartment and pulled out the gun he always carried with him. As quietly as possible, he climbed from the truck and walked toward the entrance.

At the door he stood to one side and slowly pulled it open. Seeing and hearing no one, he slipped into the arena. Rows of bleachers faced the livestock paneling that enclosed the practice area, and he moved stealthily down the aisle between two sections. He was almost to the fence when he spotted her. She was positioned just as she had been in the picture—in a chair in the middle of the arena, her hands tied behind her back.

Dean glanced around again, but saw no one. He tucked his gun into the waistband of his jeans and, moving as quickly as possible, ran to the fence, stuck his foot between two horizontal planks and hoisted himself over the paneling into the arena.

Gwen looked up when she heard his feet hit the

ground. A terrified expression flashed across her face. "Dean, get out of here before he kills you, too!"

"Not without you," he answered as he ran toward her.

He rounded her chair and stared down at her hands, which were bound with zip ties. "Who did this?" he asked as he pulled out his pocketknife.

"Billy Champion," she gasped. "But he's really Aaron King. He's Trip King's father, and this whole thing has been about getting revenge because you killed his son."

Dean sliced through the zip ties, grabbed her by the arms and pulled her from the chair. "Where is he?"

She glanced at the chute at the end of the arena. "He's gone to let Renegade out. He said he was going to put some sharp objects under the flank strap to make him wilder than usual."

She'd barely uttered the words before Dean heard a laugh echo through the enclosed area. He turned toward the chute and spotted Billy Champion, or rather Aaron King, sitting atop the fence beside the gate. "I see you made it, Dean," he yelled. "Well, I've seen to it that you and your lovely wife will have a wonderful time with an old friend of mine. I'm sure Renegade will entertain you royally."

The gate to the chute swung open, and a bull charged into the arena. Dean had never seen Renegade before, but he'd heard some of his ranch hands who competed in bull-riding events talk about him. He was even fiercer than Dean had imagined.

Renegade was one of the largest bulls he had ever seen. His large bony head and his legs were white, contrasting with the rest of his body, and his sharp horns fanned outward in a flat arc instead of a lyre shape. But this animal's reputation had nothing to do with the way he looked. It was the way he moved. And today he moved like a whirlwind.

Snorting and bucking, Renegade spun in circles as soon as he entered the arena. His back hooves sent swirls of dirt flying as he kicked and writhed in an attempt to free the flank strap that evidently was causing him pain.

Dean grabbed Gwen by the arm and ran toward the fence. "You've got to get over before he charges us!" he yelled.

The words were no sooner out of his mouth than the bull spotted them and charged. His thundering hooves echoed in the quiet building as Dean and Gwen ran for their lives.

They reached the fence, but Renegade was almost on them. Gwen thrust her foot in the space between two planks, and Dean hoisted her up. She lifted her other leg and slung it over the top plank. "Drop to the ground! I'll distract him!" Dean yelled as he turned and ran back toward the center of the arena.

Renegade, who'd been bearing down on them, turned immediately and dashed after him. Dean glanced back over his shoulder and saw that Gwen had dropped safely on the other side of the fence. Renegade was right behind him, and he could almost feel the bull's hot breath on his back.

Dean sidestepped, but the huge animal lowered his head and swung his horns perilously close to him. With all his might, Dean landed a punch on the bull's nose and then slid his hand along Renegade's back until he reached the slipknot holding the flank strap in place. With a quick jerk on the rope, the strap fell to the ground, and Renegade slowed some, giving Dean a split second to sprint toward the fence Gwen had climbed over.

The reprieve was short, however, because a moment later, Renegade bellowed in rage once more and charged after him. Dean had just reached the fence when Renegade caught up with him. Lowering his head, the bull gored him, slicing through his jeans and down his leg as he climbed over. Bleeding and winded, Dean dropped to the ground, where he lay panting.

"Dean!" Gwen cried, dropping to her knees beside him. "Where did he hurt you?"

Dean grabbed his knee and pressed down. "My lower leg. Get the bandanna out of my pocket. I need to get a tourniquet on this."

Her fingers shook as she pulled the scarf from his back pocket and tied it around his leg just below the kneecap. When she'd pulled it as tight as she could, he pushed himself to his feet. "You've got to get out of here, and I've got to find Billy."

She shook her head. "I'm not leaving you."

Dean swayed as if he was about to fall and reached out to grab hold of the fence. "Ben is on his way with backup. He and his deputies should be here any minute, and I want you out of here." He straightened and grasped her arm.

"No. You're hurt," she protested.

He tightened his grip on her and turned her to face him. "Listen to me, Gwen. I need you to get in my truck. Stay there until I come back or until Ben arrives. If you see Billy, you are to drive out of here as fast as you can. Do you hear me?"

"Yes, but…"

He gritted his teeth and stared at her. "I have to know you're safe."

Her eyes softened, and she reached up and cupped his face with her hand. "Be careful. We need you."

He swallowed the lump in his throat and nodded. "And I need you and Maggie, too."

Gwen wrapped her arm around his waist and supported his weight as they staggered toward the door he had entered. When they stepped outside, he pulled his keys from his pocket and handed them to her. "Lock yourself in the truck, and get out of here if you see Billy."

She bit her lip and nodded. "I will."

Then she released him and ran toward the vehicle. Dean watched until she had got inside. Then he pulled the gun from the back of his jeans and turned to reenter the arena. He had no idea where Billy was, but intended to find him and make sure the man was taken into custody before he could hurt anyone else. Under no circumstances would Dean allow Billy to harm Gwen again.

THIRTEEN

Dean eased the door to the arena open and slipped through the opening. He stopped just inside and glanced down at his leg. Blood soaked his jeans, and he could feel it trickling down his calf. He only hoped the tourniquet would slow the flow long enough for him to find Billy.

As he moved down the aisle, Dean scanned the building for any sign of him, but saw nothing. Renegade, calmer than he'd been earlier, stared at him through the galvanized panels that encircled the practice area. His tail swished back and forth, and he pawed at the ground as if inviting Dean to give him one more chance to finish what he'd started.

When Dean got to the front row of bleachers, he hesitated and looked to the left, then the right. His gaze settled on the chute at the far end where Renegade had been before Billy released him. Animal pens behind the chutes offered good hiding places. The question was, which way should Dean go first?

After a moment's hesitation, he turned left in the

direction of Renegade's chute. Like a hulking shadow, the bull walked along the other side of the fence as Dean made his way toward the far end of the arena. From time to time Renegade swiveled his head and lunged at the barrier, the sound of the impact ricocheting around the arena.

Dean kept his eyes focused ahead and tried to ignore the pain in his leg. The bleachers ended at a door that he remembered from a previous visit opened onto an alleyway between rows of pens. He pulled the door slightly open, but before he could get it wide enough to walk through, it flew back, hitting him and knocking him to the ground.

Dean fell in front of the first row of bleachers, his gun dropping from his hand and landing a few feet away. He looked up to see Billy Champion lunging through the door at him. The expression on his face made him look like a madman, and Dean knew he had to get up if he was to survive the attack. He tried to push himself up, but it was no use. Billy landed on top of him and grasped his throat in a choke hold. Dean grabbed Billy's shirt in his fists and tried to push him off, but the man only increased the pressure on Dean's throat.

"It's time you paid for killing my son!" he yelled as he tightened his hands around Dean's neck.

"Billy…" Dean panted.

"Aaron!" he screamed. "My name is Aaron King, father of Trip King. The man you killed. And I'm going to make you pay!"

The veins in Aaron's neck bulged as he leaned

closer to Dean until their foreheads almost touched. Dean raised his hands, grasped the man's face and squeezed with all his might. His nemesis groaned and loosened his grip a bit.

Remembering his training as a police officer, Dean slid his fingers up Aaron's face to the top of his cheekbones. Then he slipped his thumbs in his eyes and pushed with all his strength. The man gave a wail of distress, released his hold on Dean's throat and jerked away.

Dean seized the moment to draw back a fist and land a hard blow to his jaw. Aaron toppled off him onto his back. As Dean struggled to get up, his opponent jumped to his feet and kicked his leg where the bull had gored him.

"Aghhh!" Dean cried out in pain, grabbed at his leg and fell backward.

From the corner of his eye, he spotted his gun lying a few feet away. Aaron aimed another blow at his leg, but Dean rolled over, avoiding the kick, and grabbed his weapon. Sucking in a breath, he summoned what little strength he had left, sat up and pointed the gun at Aaron, who took one step toward him, then stopped.

"It's over, Aaron," Dean barked. "Come any closer and I'll fire."

Aaron let his gaze drop to the gun Dean held and then shook his head. "And what will you do if I go the other way instead? You have to catch me first, and it doesn't look like you're in any condition to come after me," he snarled.

With that, he turned, took a flying leap and scaled the fence into the arena. Dean pushed himself to his feet and stumbled to the paneling. "Come back, Aaron. Renegade's still in there."

Aaron hesitated a moment as he turned and stared at the big bull, who stood pawing at the ground, his head lowered. A flicker of surprise crossed the man's face. It seemed he'd forgotten Renegade's presence. He looked back the way he'd come, but clearly realized Dean would capture him if he returned. Then he sprinted for the fence at the far side of the arena.

But Renegade was faster. He charged at Aaron and, with seemingly little effort, caught up with the man. The bull bellowed as he lowered his head and speared him in the back with one of his horns, then lifted him and tossed him through the air, sending him crashing to the ground on the other side of the fence.

Renegade continued to butt his head against the paneling as if challenging Aaron to get up, but Dean didn't see any movement. He wanted to go to him, see if he was alive, but didn't think he could make his legs move. A dizzy feeling overtook him, and he collapsed back onto the ground just as he heard the outside door crash open.

"Dean!" Ben called out. "Are you in here?"

He swallowed and forced himself to answer. "Over here, Ben," he wheezed.

Dean looked up to see his friend and two deputies bending over him. Ben took one look at his jeans and glanced at one of the men. "Call 911. We need an ambulance right away." He leaned closer. "Gwen told me about Billy. Where is he?"

Dean tried to raise his hand to point to the other side of the arena, but it wouldn't cooperate. "Over there," he whispered. "See if he's still alive."

The two deputies nodded and hurried off toward the other side, one of them on the radio with Dispatch, giving an update about the situation and the number of ambulances to send. Ben put his hand on Dean's shoulder and squeezed. "Hang on, buddy. There's medical help on the way."

Before Dean could respond, he heard the door open again and Gwen's voice cry out, "Dean, where are you?"

"Over here," Ben yelled.

Then she was beside him. Dean looked up into the eyes that had first made his heart pound the night they'd met. They were filled with tears now, just like then. "Don't cry, Gwen," he whispered. "I'm going to be okay."

He saw her lips move and knew she must be saying something, but he couldn't hear. He felt the darkness closing in as his eyes drifted shut.

Gwen grabbed Dean's hand and clasped it in both of hers. His fingers felt like ice, and she rubbed them as she sobbed. "Dean, I love you! Don't leave me!"

She felt strong hands grasp her shoulders, and she gazed up into Ben's face. He looked as scared as she felt, but somehow he managed to smile. "He's going to be all right, Gwen. The paramedics will be here any minute. Just keep talking to him. Maybe he can hear what you're saying."

She looked back down at Dean as words began to pour from her mouth. She didn't know what she was saying or if it even made sense, but for the next few minutes she told him everything she could about Maggie—how she could eat macaroni and cheese for every meal, how she couldn't stand the taste of asparagus. Her favorite color was red. Her favorite flower was a daisy. How she loved to draw, and how she was going to love looking at the night sky from the front porch at Little Pigeon Ranch.

Gwen babbled until her throat became raspy, but she didn't stop, determined to reach him with her words and remind him of all he had to live for.

Suddenly Ben touched her shoulder again and leaned toward her. "The EMTs are coming in the door, Gwen. You need to get up now and let them do their job."

She gave Dean's hand one last squeeze before she rose to her feet and backed away as four paramedics rushed into the building. Her heart gave a little leap when she recognized Joe, the EMT who'd taken care of her in the ambulance after she had almost been killed. That was only a few short days ago, but so much had happened since then that it seemed a lifetime.

Joe smiled at her. "Miss Anderson, we meet again. But this time it's Dean who needs attention. Don't worry. We'll take good care of him." He glanced at Ben. "We were told there were two victims. Where's the other one?"

Ben nodded toward the other side of the arena. "He's over there. It's Billy Champion, or I should say Aaron King. Two of my deputies are with him and they tell me he's badly hurt. He was gored through the side by that bull in the arena. One of the horns caught Dean in the leg."

Two of the paramedics headed to Aaron, while Joe and the other one dropped down on opposite sides of Dean and started their examination. Gwen could hardly breathe as she watched Joe cut Dean's jeans away from the wound and begin emergency treatment. After a few minutes he glanced up at her.

"He's lost quite a bit of blood. We need to get him to the hospital." Joe glanced at Ben. "We brought two ambulances, so we'll transport them separately."

He nodded. "My deputies and I will help any way we can."

At that moment one of the paramedics called across from the other side, "We need to get a gurney over here. I'll bring an ambulance around here so we can load him."

"We'll load Dean from this side. See you at the hospital."

The EMT with Joe jumped up, dashed out the door and was back within a minute rolling a gurney. "Okay, Joe," he said, "you grab him by the shoulders, and I'll get his legs. Let's be careful with that limb. We don't need that wound to open up even more."

When they had Dean settled on the gurney, they hustled toward the exit and then the ambulance. Gwen followed as quickly as she could, and when they stepped out into the sunlight, she could see how pale Dean was. What if he died? How could she ever forgive herself if that happened and she had to live with the guilt that she had robbed him of five years he could have had with his daughter? And poor Maggie would never get a chance to know the wonderful father who would have loved her so much. Hot tears flooded her eyes once again.

She felt Ben's arm wrap around her shoulders as they stopped at the back of the ambulance. "Don't worry, Gwen," he said. "I've known Dean a long time. He's a tough guy. It'll take more than a seventeen-hundred-pound bull to get the best of him."

She looked up into Ben's face and smiled. "Thank you. Are you going to the hospital?"

"I'll be there as soon as I can. First of all, I have to call Mr. Lambert. He needs to get some cowboys over here to take care of Renegade. Then I'll make sure Dean's truck is delivered back to the ranch and check on your car in the tunnel, see if my other deputies have had it towed into town."

Her eyes widened in surprise. "How did you know my car was in the tunnel?"

"Dean found it. He was trying to catch up with you before you could get on a plane back to New York. He called me as soon as he spotted your abandoned car, and then he got that text."

Her heart fluttered, and she gazed into the back of the ambulance, where Joe and the other paramedic were getting Dean situated for the ride to the hospital. "Then he must not have wanted me to leave," she said.

Ben shook his head. "I expect he didn't. All he's talked about for the last five years was how much he loved you and how he had messed up your marriage. But from what he told me last night, he wasn't the only one who made mistakes."

Gwen's eyes welled up again. "No, he wasn't."

Ben smiled. "Then it looks like God had a plan to bring you two back together. Now go take care of Dean while I finish up my work here."

She put her arms around Ben and gave him a brief hug. "Thanks for being such a good friend."

"Oh, I didn't do anything except pray for the two of you. Be happy, Gwen."

"I will."

At that moment one of the EMTs jumped out of the rear of the ambulance and ran around to the driver's side. Joe stepped to the back door and looked down at her. "Miss Anderson, do you want to ride with Dean?"

Suddenly Gwen realized she had to make a decision that would impact the lives of Dean, Maggie and her. When she'd left this morning, she had believed that she'd ruined any chance of happiness with him, but then he had come after her. Did that mean he wanted a life for the three of them? Was that what *she* wanted?

They'd tried marriage once before and had failed. Now they had Maggie, and if they weren't successful a second time, she would be hurt, too. What was the best choice for all three of them?

"I certainly do," Gwen said. "He's my husband."

Ben took her hand and helped her climb up into the ambulance. She settled beside Dean for the ride to the hospital. As the vehicle pulled out of the parking lot, she bowed her head. *Dear God,* she prayed, *watch over Dean and heal him. Please give us another chance to make our marriage work so that we can be parents to our daughter, and man and wife together, the way You intended. Just one more chance, one more.*

She mumbled the prayer over and over all the way to the hospital, the entire time Dean was being examined by doctors, and then throughout the hours he was in surgery before he was finally moved to the recovery room. She had dreaded being alone while she waited, but she needn't have worried about that. Within minutes after her arrival at the hospital, Shorty, along with several employees from the ranch, crowded through the door and dropped down on the couches and chairs to wait for word of the man they respected as a boss and valued as a friend. Concern lined their faces, and it made her feel good to know that the men who worked for Dean regarded him so highly.

Time seemed to drag by, and the mood in the waiting room grew more somber by the minute. To distract herself, Gwen began to mull over the events of the past few days and began to realize that a simple decision Dean had made years ago had created a chain reaction that almost ended in another tragedy today.

She remembered that night Dean had told her he wasn't supposed to be on duty, but was going to take a fellow officer's shift so the man could be at the hospital with his sick child. Good-hearted intentions, but they had put him in Trip's path and had led to Trip's death as well as the death of a good friend of Dean's.

Unable to deal with the self-imposed guilt of killing a young man, Dean had turned to alcohol to dim his thoughts, and that decision had ultimately brought about the end of their marriage. Dean's inability to cope with his problems had caused her to keep the existence of his child a secret. Meanwhile, Aaron's anger and bitterness had festered, driving him toward plans of revenge. All of them had lived half lives for years as they struggled to cope with the memories of the past.

But that time was over now. Dean had come after her when she'd left, so that must mean he still loved her. And he had put himself at risk today to save her life. They had a future together, and she intended to do everything she could to make it happen.

"Gwen." The sound of her name being called pulled her from her thoughts, and she looked up to see Ben standing in front of her, his big Stetson hat in his hand. "Have you heard anything?"

She stood and shook her head. "Not yet, but it should be anytime now. It feels like he's been in surgery for hours."

She'd no sooner finished speaking than the doctor walked into the room. He pulled off the surgical cap he still wore and smiled as he came toward her. "Miss Anderson, I wanted to let you know that Dean came through the surgery successfully. There was some damage to the leg, and he's going to need some physical therapy. But the good news is he's going to be fine."

Gwen turned to the ranch employees, who had all got to their feet when the doctor walked in. "Did you hear that? Dean is going to be fine."

The tension they'd been radiating dissolved with a collective sigh of relief. They grinned at each other, but Shorty swiped at his eyes. "That's good news, Miss Gwen. Good news indeed."

"What about Mr. King?" Ben asked.

The doctor exhaled and shook his head. "He was more badly injured than Dean. He had a punctured lung, but we think he'll recover."

Ben's face hardened. "Good. He needs to stand trial for all the things he's done. I'll have to post a deputy here to guard him until he's well enough to be taken to jail."

The doctor nodded. "I understand. I'll take you to meet the head of our security so you can work out the details." He turned back to Gwen. "Do you have any more questions?"

"Yes. I wanted to ask about Dean's foreman, Emmett Truitt. How is he doing?"

"He's doing fine. I checked on him earlier, and he was fussing because he had to stay another day here."

Gwen smiled as she envisioned a frustrated Emmett wanting to be up and on his horse again. "I'll go see him later. When can I see Dean?"

"He's in recovery now, but we'll be moving him to a room in an hour or so. I'll have the nurse come get you, and you can stay as long as you like. He'll be sedated for a while, so don't expect to talk with him until morning. He should be awake then."

For the first time in days Gwen felt as if a heavy burden had been lifted from her shoulders. She smiled and shook the doctor's hand. "Thank you."

"I'm glad I could be of service and glad it turned out so well for my patient. Now, you have a good night, and I'll see you tomorrow. If all goes well, you may get to take him home, but he's going to be incapacitated for a while."

"That's no problem," Gwen said. "Between the men who work at Little Pigeon Ranch and me, we'll see that he's well cared for."

The doctor smiled and glanced at Ben. "If you'll follow me, I'll take you to meet our security chief now."

Ben nodded. "I'll see you later, Gwen. When Dean wakes up, tell him I'll see him tomorrow." He started to leave, then stopped and turned back to her. "By the way, I received word before I got here that the state lab had phoned. They're releasing James's body tomorrow. So tell Dean he can go ahead and plan his grandfather's funeral. If he needs me to help, I'm there for him."

"Thanks, Ben. I'll tell him."

Shorty stepped up beside her. "Don't worry, Miss

Gwen. We're all here to help Dean during this rough time, but we need to get on back to the ranch now if you think you'll be all right by yourself. We've got chores to do before dark. Dean wouldn't want us hanging around here and lettin' his animals go hungry."

Gwen chuckled as she gave the cook a quick hug. "Go on. I'll call in the morning and let you know how Dean and Emmett are. Hopefully, we'll have both of them home soon. Then we can plan James's funeral."

Shorty nodded and took her hand in his. "That sounds almost like you're beginning to think of the Little Pigeon as your home, too."

A warm feeling engulfed her at the kindness shining in his eyes, and she realized it really was her home now—hers and Maggie's. "I can't imagine anywhere I'd rather be, Shorty."

"That's good news," he said. "James would be mighty proud you were coming home. That's what he always wanted."

She swallowed the lump in her throat and shook hands with the men as they filed by one by one. Then she was alone.

A while later a nurse came for her, and Gwen followed her to Dean's darkened room. "Call if you need anything," she said before she hurried away.

Gwen nodded and stared down at Dean, whose chest rose and fell in a steady rhythm. After several minutes she pulled a chair to his bedside, covered his hand with hers and settled in to keep watch. She had wasted too many years, and if he'd let her, she was going to be with him the rest of her life.

It's going to be a long night, she thought as she waited to find out whether he wanted the same things she did.

FOURTEEN

For a moment when Gwen opened her eyes, she couldn't remember where she was, but then it came to her. She was in Dean's hospital room, and she'd been asleep with her head resting on the side of his bed. She felt a hand caress her hair, and she slowly sat up. Dean stared at her as his palm slid down the back of her head to the side of her face. He trailed his fingers across her cheek and grazed his thumb across her lips.

"Good morning." His voice sounded very much like the croak of a frog, and she couldn't help but smile.

"Good morning to you, too," she said. "How are you feeling this morning?"

"Hungry. I have a craving for some of Shorty's pancakes. How about you?"

Her stomach growled in answer, and she laughed. "I guess I'm hungry, too. Come to think of it, I didn't have dinner last night."

His eyes darkened, and he frowned. "Were you here all night?"

She nodded. "Yes, I didn't want to leave you alone. I had company for a while. Ben was here, as well as Shorty and some of the ranch hands. And a couple I hadn't met before—Steve and Betty Price—heard you'd been hurt, and they came by to check on you after everyone had left. They said to tell you their son, Jason, was going to be fine and that they'd be praying for you."

"I'm so glad to hear that. I met them in the waiting room while I was here with Emmett," Dean murmured. The hand that had been caressing her face slipped to the back of her neck, tightened and pulled her head closer. "I'm so glad *you* weren't hurt. I nearly died when I got that picture of you, and then when I saw you in that arena…"

She put a finger on his lips to silence him. "Don't think about that now. Let's be thankful that it all turned out well for us. We made it through, and the doctor says you're going to be all right. You're going to have to take it easy for a while, but I've promised him that I'll take good care of you."

Dean's eyes searched her face as if he was trying to determine if she was being truthful. "Does that mean you're thinking about staying?"

"Only if you want me to."

His Adam's apple bobbed, and his eyes sparkled. "If I want you to? My prayer for the last five years has been that God would bring you back to me. Then when He did and you told me about Maggie, I made a mess of everything. I'm so sorry."

Gwen shook her head. "No, it was my fault. I was wrong not to tell you about Maggie years ago. Can you ever forgive me for that?"

His hand stroked across her back and up again to her neck. "Both of us made mistakes. I've already forgiven you for keeping her a secret, but I need to know if you can forgive me and trust that I will never, ever put you or our child through the agony that I did when we were married. I love you, Gwen, and I want you with me. Marry me again, and let's spend the rest of our lives making up for the years we've lost."

Her heart pounded in her chest, and she smiled through her tears. "I've always loved you, Dean, and I want to be your wife again. But I have to warn you. Your life is about to change drastically. Living with two females in the house can be a challenging experience. Are you sure you're up to it?"

He grinned up at her. "I think a guy who has taken on a raging bull and lived to tell about it is up to the challenge. Bring it on."

Then he pulled her down to him until their lips met. Gwen framed his face between her hands as his arms circled her. They clung together, pouring all the loneliness and hurt of the past five years into their kiss.

When they finally pulled apart, Dean smoothed Gwen's hair back from her face and stared into her eyes. "For the last five years I've lived a half life. I've been adrift without hope that we could ever be together again. God's given us a second chance at happiness. I realize what a precious gift that is, and I promise I'll be worthy of you."

"And I of you," she said as she lowered her lips to his again.

Three weeks later Dean, Ben and Emmett sat on the front porch, staring down the driveway for the first sign of Gwen's car. Although he'd wanted her to fly from New York, she'd insisted on driving because she wanted to bring her car. But where was she? It had been an hour since she'd called and said they were headed toward the ranch. Dean was growing more impatient by the minute.

"Did Gwen get everything taken care of in New York?" Emmett asked, without taking his eyes off the road.

Dean nodded. "Yeah, but she had a lot to do. It's not easy packing up all your belongings and moving to another part of the country. She had to decide what she wanted to put in storage and what she wanted to bring here. Plus she had to give the network two weeks' notice and finish out her work there."

"Sounds like she's been busy," Ben said.

Dean glanced down at his leg and frowned. "Yeah, and I should have been there helping her, but she insisted I stay for my physical therapy."

"She was right about that. I can tell you're getting better every time you go. Besides, I want you to be able to walk down the aisle without a cane at your wedding, and you haven't got much time left before the big day."

"I can't believe it's this weekend," Dean said. They had talked about getting married before Gwen went back to New York, but had ultimately concluded that they wanted Maggie to be present. So they'd decided to wait until Gwen had settled all her affairs back East, which included getting her mother on board with their decision to remarry.

Thankfully, that hadn't been as difficult as they'd feared. She loved Gwen and Maggie and wanted them to be happy. She was flying in the day before the wedding.

"It's gonna be different having two women around the ranch," Emmett said. "You think your daughter is gonna like it?"

Dean wiped at the perspiration that popped out on his head. "I don't know. Gwen assures me that she will. Of course, it's going to be different than city life."

Ben waved his hand in dismissal. "She's gonna love it here. What kid wouldn't? Besides, with a mother like Gwen, she'll adapt in no time."

Emmett nodded. "Yeah. That Gwen is something else. I never will forget how she saved my life that day at Rattlesnake Creek. She fired that gun like she was a pro. And the funeral she planned for James was a real tribute to his life." He stretched his legs out in front of him and sighed. "Yeah, I think it's going to be great having two females around."

"It will be if they ever get here," Dean said as he glanced down at his watch. "Where could they be?

It's been over an hour since she called to say she was almost here."

Ben and Emmett looked at each other and chuckled. "Relax," Ben said. "You know the roads are always crowded with tourist traffic this time of day. They'll get here soon."

Dean turned an anxious glance in Ben's direction. "What if Maggie doesn't like me?"

Emmett laughed and wagged his head. "Don't go looking for trouble before she even gets here. She's gonna love you."

Dean started to speak, but a car turned off the road at that moment and began the drive up the lane. Dean straightened to his full height, grabbed his cane and hobbled down the steps with Ben and Emmett following. Behind him Dean heard the front door open. He turned to see Shorty coming onto the porch. All three men looked as anxious as Dean felt. He took a deep breath as the car pulled to a stop in front of them.

Gwen jumped out on the driver's side and ran around to where they stood. "This is quite a welcoming committee. It's good to see all of you." She gave Dean a swift kiss on the cheek and stared into his eyes. "Are you ready?"

He swallowed and nodded. "I haven't slept in a week thinking about what this moment is going to be like."

Smiling, she stepped back to the car and opened the back door. Dean tried to see the child buckled in the safety seat, but Gwen blocked his view. He heard the click of the restraints as she released them, and then a child's voice drifted from the car. "Is my daddy here, Mommy?"

"Yes, darling. He's waiting to meet you."

Dean's throat closed up, and his chest tightened so much he didn't think he could breathe as Gwen stepped back and helped the most beautiful child he'd ever seen climb from the backseat. He almost gasped at the first sight of her.

Gwen had been right. Maggie's hair was the same shade as hers, but their daughter's eyes were identical to the ones that stared back at him from the mirror every morning. She wore a red dress with white polka dots, and her ponytail was tied with a red bow. When she smiled at him, dimples creased her cheeks as if they were extending a welcome just for him.

For a moment he felt as if his breath had been stolen from him, and then he moved toward her. He wanted to wrap his arms around her, but didn't want to scare her. He held his hand out to her, and she looked up at her mother. Gwen nodded and gave her a little nudge in the back, and Maggie took a step toward him.

Ignoring the pain in his leg, he dropped to his knees and smiled at her. "Hello, Maggie. I'm so glad to meet you."

She stared at him a minute, as if unsure what to do. Then she put her hand in his. His heart raced as he closed his big fingers around her small ones. "Are you really my daddy?" she asked, tilting her head to one side.

He cleared his throat and nodded. "I am. I'm sorry I haven't gotten to meet you before."

She smiled, and his heart skipped a beat. "Mommy said you had to be away from us because you had important work to do."

He glanced up at Gwen, who was staring down at both of them, and she nodded. That was the explanation they had decided to tell Maggie now. His important work had been trying to reclaim his life from alcoholism, and he'd accomplished that. When Maggie was older, they would tell her the full truth, but for now they needed to start rebuilding their family.

"Yes, Maggie. I had important work to do, but that's all over now. It's time for you, your mommy and me to be a family."

She sighed. "I'm glad, Daddy. I've missed you."

Before he knew what was happening, she had thrown her arms around his neck and was hugging him with all her might. He turned his mouth to her cheek and kissed her. "I've missed you, too, darling, but I'm here now. Welcome to Little Pigeon Ranch."

After a moment she pulled back and stared at him, an excited look on her face. "Mommy said you have puppies. Can I see them?"

"Of course you can. Sadie has been waiting to meet you and let you pick out the one that's going to be your very own."

Her eyes grew wide. "Really, Daddy? I'm going to get a puppy?"

He smiled. "Of course you are. All girls who live on a ranch need a dog, and a horse, as well. I'm going to teach you to ride, and your mommy and I are going to take you on trail rides all over these mountains."

Maggie's face grew animated, and she squealed in delight as she turned to her mother. "Mommy, did you hear? I'm going to have a puppy *and* a horse."

Gwen smiled and wiped the corner of her eye. "I heard. That sounds wonderful."

Behind him Dean heard a sniffle, but he didn't turn around to see how his friends were dealing with the scene that had just played out. It was enough that they were here with him today to witness this reunion. His only regret was that his grandfather wasn't, but the love he had given Dean still lived in the house James had built for his wife so many years ago. He'd be happy to know that his prayers had been answered—to have the next generation of the Harwell family living on the ranch he'd loved so much.

Gwen dropped on her knees and leaned toward him. Dean kept one arm around Maggie and wrapped the other around Gwen, then pulled them both against him. He closed his eyes for a moment, said a silent prayer of thanks and asked God to bless their family.

"I love you both," he whispered. "Welcome home."

* * * * *

If you loved this story, don't miss these other great reads by Sandra Robbins:

FUGITIVE TRACKDOWN
FUGITIVE AT LARGE
YULETIDE FUGITIVE THREAT

Dear Reader,

Ever since I wrote *Final Warning*, my first book for Love Inspired Suspense, I have had emails from readers wanting to know when I was going to write the story of Dean and Gwen, secondary characters in that book. I have honored that request by writing *In a Killer's Sights*. It is a story set against the majestic Smoky Mountains and tells of a deep love marred by problems of alcoholism and hidden secrets. When all seems hopeless, Dean and Gwen find the solution to their problems lies in turning to God and putting their trust in Him. Only God can make our lives, which are stained with sin, be washed clean and become as white as snow.

If you are burdened by problems and unsure what to do, I pray you will put your trust in God to deliver you to a new life. He can return you to peace and joy.

Sandra Robbins

COMING NEXT MONTH FROM
Love Inspired® Suspense

Available August 2, 2016

SECRETS AND LIES
Rookie K-9 Unit • by Shirlee McCoy
When someone tries to kill pregnant teacher Ariel Martin at the local high school, her student's brother, K-9 officer Tristan McKeller, saves her. But can he unravel the secrets in the single mother's past and discover who's after her?

SILENT SABOTAGE
First Responders • by Susan Sleeman
Emily Graves moves to a small town to take over her aunt's bed-and-breakfast...and finds her life in jeopardy. Now if she wants to survive—and save the family business—Emily must turn to Deputy Sheriff Archer Reed for protection.

FATAL VENDETTA • by Sharon Dunn
While reporting on a fire, television journalist Elizabeth Kramer is kidnapped. And with the help of her rival, blogger Zachery Beck, she escapes. Now, as Elizabeth's stalker becomes increasingly violent, Zach is determined to keep her safe.

PLAIN COVER-UP • by Alison Stone
Taking a leave from his job, FBI agent Dylan Hunter expects a chance to relax in a small Amish community—until his former love, Christina Jennings, is attacked. Somebody wants her dead...and she needs his help to stay alive.

DEAD END • by Lisa Phillips
Former CIA agent Nina Holmes is determined to find her mother's killer. And when her investigation puts Nina in danger, she and US marshal Wyatt Ames must solve the murder...or Nina could become a serial killer's next victim.

RANCH REFUGE
Rangers Under Fire • by Virginia Vaughan
When former army ranger Colton Blackwell saves Laura Jackson from an attempted kidnapping, he takes her to his ranch for safety. But when the loan shark trying to collect on her father's debt sends attackers from all directions, will Colton's protection be enough?

LISCNM0716

REQUEST YOUR FREE BOOKS!
2 FREE RIVETING INSPIRATIONAL NOVELS
PLUS 2 FREE MYSTERY GIFTS

Love Inspired®
SUSPENSE
RIVETING INSPIRATIONAL ROMANCE

YES! Please send me 2 FREE Love Inspired® Suspense novels and my 2 FREE mystery gifts (gifts are worth about $10). After receiving them, if I don't wish to receive any more books, I can return the shipping statement marked "cancel." If I don't cancel, I will receive 4 brand-new novels every month and be billed just $4.99 per book in the U.S. or $5.49 per book in Canada. That's a savings of at least 17% off the cover price. It's quite a bargain! Shipping and handling is just 50¢ per book in the U.S. and 75¢ per book in Canada.* I understand that accepting the 2 free books and gifts places me under no obligation to buy anything. I can always return a shipment and cancel at any time. Even if I never buy another book, the two free books and gifts are mine to keep forever.

123/323 IDN GH5Z

Name _____ (PLEASE PRINT) _____

Address _____ Apt. # _____

City _____ State/Prov. _____ Zip/Postal Code _____

Signature (if under 18, a parent or guardian must sign) _____

Mail to the **Reader Service:**
IN U.S.A.: P.O. Box 1867, Buffalo, NY 14240-1867
IN CANADA: P.O. Box 609, Fort Erie, Ontario L2A 5X3

Are you a current subscriber to Love Inspired® Suspense books
and want to receive the larger-print edition?
Call 1-800-873-8635 or visit www.ReaderService.com.

* Terms and prices subject to change without notice. Prices do not include applicable taxes. Sales tax applicable in N.Y. Canadian residents will be charged applicable taxes. Offer not valid in Quebec. This offer is limited to one order per household. Not valid for current subscribers to Love Inspired Suspense books. All orders subject to credit approval. Credit or debit balances in a customer's account(s) may be offset by any other outstanding balance owed by or to the customer. Please allow 4 to 6 weeks for delivery. Offer available while quantities last.

Your Privacy—The Reader Service is committed to protecting your privacy. Our Privacy Policy is available online at www.ReaderService.com or upon request from the Reader Service.
We make a portion of our mailing list available to reputable third parties that offer products we believe may interest you. If you prefer that we not exchange your name with third parties, or if you wish to clarify or modify your communication preferences, please visit us at www.ReaderService.com/consumerchoice or write to us at Reader Service Preference Service, P.O. Box 9062, Buffalo, NY 14240-9062. Include your complete name and address.

LIS15

Glass shattering.

Rookie K-9 officer Tristan McKeller heard it as he hooked his K-9 partner to a lead. The yellow Lab cocked his head to the side, growling softly.

"What is it, boy?" Tristan asked, scanning the school parking lot. Only one other vehicle was parked there—a shiny black minivan that he knew belonged to Ariel Martin, the teacher he was supposed be meeting with. He was late. Of course. That seemed to be the story of his life this summer. Work was crazy, and his sister was crazier, and finding time to meet with her summer-school teacher? He'd already canceled two previous meetings. He couldn't cancel this one. Not if Mia had any hope of getting through summer school.

He was going to be even later than he'd anticipated, though, because Jesse was still growling, alerted to something that must have to do with the shattering glass.

"Find!" he commanded, and Jesse took off, pulling against the leash in his haste to get to the corner of the building and around it. Trained in arson detection, the dog had an unerring nose for almost anything. Right now, he was on a scent, and Tristan trusted him enough to let him have his head.

Glass glittered on the pavement twenty feet away, and Jesse beelined for it, barking raucously, his tail stiff and high.

A woman appeared in the window. Dark hair. Pale skin. Freckles. Very pregnant belly that wasn't cooperating as she struggled to crawl through the opening. Ariel Martin. The newest teacher at Desert Valley High School. Smart. Enthusiastic. Patient. He'd heard that from more than one parent. He'd even heard it from Mia.

"You okay?" he asked, running to her side.

She shook her head, dark gray eyes wide with shock, a smear of blood on her right hand. She'd cut herself. It looked deep, but she didn't seem to notice. "He's got a gun. He tried to shoot me."

Don't miss SECRETS AND LIES
by Shirlee McCoy, available wherever
Love Inspired® Suspense books and ebooks are sold.

www.LoveInspired.com